STRIDER'S MISSTEP

MAYHEM MAKERS

WRETCHED SOULZ MC

MANDA MELLETT

Disclaimer

This book, and the others in the Mayhem Makers series, are firmly set in the fictional world. Although the very real Motorcycles, Mobsters and Mayhem signing is mentioned, none of the events actually take place or exist outside of the author's imagination.

Please bear in mind that I've used some artistic license. Time moves differently in a fictional world. In real life there is less time between the two MMM signings, so if you're eagle eyed and spotted this, please give me a pass.

This is a work of fiction. Names, characters, businesses, places, events and incidents are either the products of the author's imagination or used in a fictitious manner. Any resemblance to actual persons, living or dead, or actual events is purely coincidental.

Warning

This book is dark in places and contains content of a sexual, abusive and violent nature. It may not be suitable for persons under the age of 18.

PRODUCTION ACKNOWLEDGMENTS

Photographer Golden Czermak

Model Victor Rahl

Cover Design by CT Cover Creations

Edited and formatted by Maggie Kern @ Ms.Kedits

Proof reading by Darlene Tallman

WRETCHED SOULZ MC

WRETCHED SOULZ MC
CHARACTER LIST

<u>*Arizona Wretched Souls Officers*</u>
Chaz – President
Bull – VP
Iron – Sergeant-at-arms
Beard – Treasurer
Weasel – Road Captain
Claw – Enforcer
Legend – IT guy

<u>*Members*</u>
Fire
Legit
Pothead
StoryTeller
Skunk

<u>*Nomads*</u>
Mac

<u>Prospects</u>
Cujo
Ryder
Shitface

<u>Texas Wretched Souls Officers</u>
Strider – President
Shotgun – VP
Buzz – Sergeant-at-arms
Shout – Secretary
Tequila – Enforcer
Data – IT guy

<u>Members</u>
Horn
Hustler
Madman
Mex
Radar
Shark

<u>Prospects</u>
Butch
Pete

DEDICATION

Strider's Misstep is dedicated to the Lowe family who lost Sherry, beloved wife/mother to Pick's Disease.
My grateful thanks go to Alex who went beyond her normal beta reader duties to revisit painful memories to go through the details of her mother's illness with me.

PROLOGUE
KATRINA

Walking into the building, I stop short when I see the main reception desk is empty, with no security guard sitting behind it. Frowning slightly, I realise that the front doors wouldn't have opened for me had my father's summons not been legit. Reasoning that today is a Sunday and that presumably his request for my attendance was on a whim, I ignore the feeling in my gut that something is wrong and head toward the elevators, choosing the one that has only one stop, the CEO's suite on the top floor.

The emptiness of the building holds no concern for me. The layout is familiar and has been so since I was seven. For the first few years of my life, where my father had disappeared during his working day was a mystery, but when the aneurysm had unexpectedly struck my mother and stolen her life, the secret had been revealed, and his workplace had become my second home. Initially struggling to immediately find arrangements for suitable childcare, the day after my mother was buried, he'd brought me with him to the office, passing me off to a frazzled assistant, leaving them to work out what to do with a grief-stricken young girl until he managed to find a live-in nanny to take care of me.

While as a child I was blind to my father's faults, after all, I'd nothing to compare him with. Even to my young mind it seemed like he was a difficult man to satisfy. Nannies came and went with singular regularity, and each time one walked out, my after-school hours and vacations were spent at a spare desk in his vast office building. I suppose it was lucky for him that I was an obedient, compliant child, content to sit with my books and games to amuse me. And as my father was, and still is, a workaholic, I saw him more at his workplace than at home.

For the past three years, this is the only place where I ever meet him. He doesn't want to interfere in my new life, or maybe it's that he doesn't want to see it up close as he knows he won't like what he would find. If we need to meet, I come to him.

I'm not complaining. There's a good reason I like it this way. This building is the one place where my security detail doesn't follow me inside. They've no need to. Barclay knows I'd never betray the only parent I have left in my life, and if I were stupid enough to take advantage of any freedom and use the opportunity to run, my escape would mean my father would die. It's the threat he's held over me since the day that I met him. Sometimes, when I don't think I can bear the way I'm forced to live any longer, the feelings I have for the man responsible for my situation turns to hate. But when all's said and done, my father is my flesh and blood, and I couldn't live with myself if any future happiness came at the price of costing him his life.

The elevator has reached the top floor as the toneless announcement informs me, and the doors take that deliberate extra moment, the one in which you have time for a second's panic as to whether you're going to be trapped before they finally deign to open with a swish.

As is the reception area below, this level is similarly empty and silent. Again, I'm reminded it's Sunday. A strange day for my father to summon me to visit, but I'm more intrigued than concerned. I haven't seen him for a couple of months. It doesn't much matter whether this is a belated catch-up or if he has something particular to tell me.

I know there are people who probably wonder how I could have ever forgiven him enough to give him the time of day. Believe me, I often ask myself that. I make the excuse for him that he had no idea what he was getting me into, his redemption that I truly don't believe he knew the depths of depravity Barclay would go to.

His office door is in front of me, and I can hear him clearing his throat inside. Before entering, I linger, my mind slipping back in time, returning to another visit I'd made to him, blissfully ignorant of the changes to come.

I all but danced up the steps into the building, thinking of the good time I'd had last night. I'd met a man I liked and who I could see becoming a boyfriend. We'd exchanged numbers and agreed to meet up., My mind elsewhere as I wonder whether I could make the first move and call him or whether propriety means I should wait for him to make contact, I automatically nod to the security guard minding the desk, smiling when he acknowledges my nonverbal greeting with a polite tilt of his chin. Still lost in my thoughts, I go to the elevator and enter, selecting the penthouse level while crossing my fingers it doesn't come to an abrupt halt between floors as it had once before. I'm not claustrophobic as such, but being trapped in a ten-by-ten box isn't my idea of fun.

Luckily, there's no such delay today, and I step out into the airy reception office, one that's large and ostentatiously decorated as befits the CEO of an international company. Gloria, my father's current receptionist, smiles at me as I approach.

I pause for a second, pulling back my shoulders and trying to focus on the here and now, putting last night out of my mind. "Is it okay for me to go straight in?" Dad might have summoned me, but that doesn't mean he hasn't been distracted by more pressing business in the meantime. I'm used to kicking my heels while waiting for him, and in preparation, I even brought a book to read.

But this time, it appears he's ready for me. "Go straight in."

I do, still with a spring in my step. That man last night was fine.

My gut clenches at the memory, at the what-might-have-beens. If only I could wave a magic wand and rewind time. I'd tell my younger self to run fast in the other direction, to never open that door.

I might only be three years older, but I feel I've aged a decade or more.

As I don't get much time to myself, getting a glimpse of my father, seeing he's bent over some paperwork on his desk, clearly engrossed, I sink down onto a seat, putting my head into my hands instead of greeting him.

How had it come to this? As I'd gotten older and seen examples of good parenting from being around my friends, I realised my father and I had never had a close relationship. Now, looking back, I can see my younger self ignoring his shortcomings. I'd lost my mom and did what I could to get the attention of my one remaining parent. Even at twenty-two years old, I was just a child yearning for familial acceptance and affection.

Ever an optimist, I was always hoping that this would be the time we'd connect on a personal level.

I'd been a straight-A student, but that was expected. I was the fruit of his loins, after all. I'd just graduated from university with a first-class honours degree in psychology. Ignoring that he'd been too busy to attend my graduation, I'd still hoped that he was proud of me. I hadn't yet decided on my future and had no idea one was already being laid out for me.

God, what a fool I'd been. Again, I let the memories overwhelm me. Going back to that time when I'd knocked on his office door, still full of innocence, my head filled with dreams of the recently met young man. Entering when his deep voice barked out permission. Closing my eyes, I go back in time, even now wondering whether there was anything I could have said or done to change things.

Stopping on the threshold, I take a moment to examine the man who created me, noticing immediately he looks different today, more dishevelled, less the totally in control businessman I'd grown used to seeing. In my gut, I already know something is wrong.

"Dad?" I say, hesitantly.

"Katrina. Come in." His voice sounds different—a little shaky, not quite sure of himself. And the glass of amber-coloured liquid instead of a cup of coffee seems wrong. It's mid-morning and normally far too early for him to be hitting the hard stuff. "Sit."

Confused and uncertain, I do as instructed, placing my butt on the visitor chair as he stands. He paces back and forth across the room a couple of times before coming to a halt in front of me. He brushes his hands back through his greying hair, then clears his throat as I wait for him to speak. His appearance and attitude are making me nervous.

He glances at me, then looks away. "Business has not been going well."

I breathe in. It's the first time he's ever discussed anything about his work. I start to wonder how bad things are, whether he's going to cut my allowance, and what I can do to help.

"I..." he coughs again. "I made some bad investments. I owe money."

I don't hesitate. "What can I do?" I've just graduated, no debts to my name as, of course, my father paid for the tuition and costs. With all the opulence surrounding him, I hadn't even thought about it twice. But now it seems maybe he overstretched himself and couldn't really afford it. I'd been selfishly taking some time to myself before entering the job market. But now I've got to think like an adult and accelerate finding employment. "I'll get a job."

He glances at me incredulously. "You wouldn't be able to earn enough." I open my mouth to protest, then shut it, knowing he's probably right and that it's only him who knows the size of the black hole in our finances. Raising his glass to his lips, he drains the liquid into his mouth, then picks up the bottle and tops off his glass. I frown, wondering when he turned to drink and worrying about the state of his liver.

After taking yet another large sip, he places the glass down. He starts to speak but only manages a squeak, then again noisily clears his throat. I fidget in my seat. He's really starting to worry me. Are we going to have to sell our house? Sure, it's ostentatious and too large for just the two of us, but it's always been home and holds memories of a happier time with my mother.

"Dad," I prompt, my voice unsteady. "How are we going to get out of this?"

His eyes narrow, his brow furrows, and he blinks rapidly. I can't remember him ever looking so sad and unsure of himself. "You're going to have to help me out. You've always been a good girl, Katrina. And now I need you to do what I ask. It's all been arranged..." His voice trails off.

After a few seconds, I encourage him again. "What has?"

There's a sinking pit in my stomach warning me I'm not going to like what I'm about to hear.

"Your marriage to Barclay Aster."

What? I'm tempted to wiggle my fingers in my ears to make sure there's nothing wrong with my hearing. But instead, I ask him to repeat himself. "What did you just say?"

His hands form fists so tight I can see his knuckles turn white. "I was looking for an investor, and Aster stepped up. But the money kept leaking out of the business. I can't afford to pay him back." Glancing at me, he then quickly turns away, as if unable to meet my eyes. "Aster's offered me a deal. He'll give me more time to pay and reduce the debt owing, but his price is you."

My mouth drops open. He's proposing to use me? "I'm not for sale." I stand, my intention to walk out the door. I'd do a lot to help my father, but sacrificing my life to an unknown man isn't the way to do it.

"Stop," he snaps with, enough authority for me to pause. "Barclay Aster isn't the man I thought he was. He's got mob connections and has threatened me and you. I've got life insurance that means he could recoup his money if I was dead, but living, I've nothing else to offer him."

The "but you" is unspoken. Nothing he says makes me feel any better. "You're giving me to a gangster?" I open my eyes wide.

Dad's words flow out fast. "He's not an actual gangster." He scoffs, but I'm not convinced of the sincerity of that statement as he continues, "In business, he's ruthless, but he's a personable man. He's promised me he'd treat you well, and I've no reason to disbelieve him."

What could I have done? Don't all children think their parents want to do their best by them? Of course, the man I'd met the night before played on my mind, but there had been no guarantee that would have gone anywhere. I'd never seen my father so distraught, and I think part of me wanted to impress him, to step up and help him out.

He'd worn me down. I'd never seen my father scared before. He'd convinced me there was no other way to save his business, and as for that threat to his life? What could I have done other than make that fatal decision when I'd agreed to at least meet Barclay?

Prior to the meeting, in my mind, I'd conjured up a man as old as the hills who wasn't able to get a woman to marry him in the normal way. But I'd been pleasantly surprised to find a man just fifteen years older than me, and much as my father had described him, a personable, affable man. He kept himself in shape and had a rugged handsomeness that wasn't unattractive. While not quick to smile, on the initial meeting, there wasn't much to complain about him. He was polite, attentive, and persuasive as he attempted to woo me. He'd successfully pulled the wool over not just my father's but my own eyes.

Against my better judgment, I gave in to Dad's pleas, but not without a few caveats and promises I made to myself. I'd gotten the contraceptive implant, which would give me three years before I had to worry about getting pregnant. That would give Dad some time to get his finances sorted out, and, if I found I couldn't love Barclay, then I could get a divorce and find a man I'd chosen for myself.

I wasn't a virgin. I hadn't been saving myself. I knew about sex or thought I had until our wedding night when I got my first glimpse of who the man I'd committed myself to really was. He was both cruel and selfish. Our intimate life was never about me and all about him.

I wanted out almost immediately. But it soon became apparent Barclay had no plans to allow me to leave. He kept me close with death threats to my father and ensured my compliance by giving me a security team that followed me wherever I went.

Except into the building my father owned. After all, Dad's existence depended on me staying Barclay's wife, so my husband knew Dad wouldn't help me escape.

I didn't pretend. Dad knew how bad my life was.

I never told Barclay I was protected about getting pregnant, even though his one goal in life apparently was to ensure that I carried his baby.

After two years, he blamed me for being barren. He punished me in a way only a cruel man like him could. He allowed any of his men who wanted to to rape me. And, of course, they all did.

Oh God. My breath catches in my chest. *How did it come to this?* There's no way out.

"Katrina?" While I'd been lost in my musings, my father had obviously finished whatever document he'd been studying and had noticed me. As I look up, his eyes shutter as he takes in the latest damage to my face that even the most expensive makeup can't cover. Barclay gave up years ago pretending he treated me with any respect.

"Have you made any progress?" The only news I want from him is that he's managed to make enough money to cover what he owes. My remaining hope is that if he repays his debt, Barclay will let me go.

His hands shake as he reaches for the inevitable glass of whisky. In the last couple of years, there's no denying he's turned to drink, verging just one step away from being an alcoholic. "He keeps adding on more interest."

I was hoping for a different response. Seeing my father as a shadow of his former self and knowing the decline in myself, I decide there's nothing to be said, and I rise and go to the door. There's nothing for me here. I might as well go.

"Wait!" He comes over and places his hand on my shoulder. Without turning me around and speaking to my back, he starts speaking fast. "There's enough cash in the safe to get you started. You can take the service lift and go out the back way. Along with the money, you'll find a set of car keys, and outside, there's a non-descript car that Barclay won't be looking for…"

What is he saying? I swing around, my mouth opening and shutting before I pull myself together enough to ask. "What are you talking about?" My brain computes his words, and I shake my head when his meaning sinks in. "I can't leave. If I go, he'll kill you."

Dad closes his eyes for a second, then leans down and places his lips to my forehead, lingering for a moment. It's a tender gesture I don't remember him doing since I was a kid. He breathes in deeply as though inhaling my perfume, then he quickly steps back. He goes behind his desk and opens a drawer, taking something out.

Before I recognise what it is or have a chance to process what's about to happen, he states, "Barclay can't threaten a dead man." He places the gun to his mouth and pulls the trigger.

A scream bursts out of my mouth. I take an automatic step forward before realising there's no helping my dad. He's slumped behind his desk. He might not be moving, but his blood is still trickling down, along with clumps of stuff I don't want to think about staining the walls.

I'm glued to the spot, my brain having difficulty processing the scene in front of me and that he's actually gone. I start to shake, and sobs rack my body as I sink to the floor, curling my knees and hugging my arms around them. Rocking back and forth, I try to make sense of what's happened here today and wait for someone to find me, to help me.

Surely someone heard me scream? That gunshot would have been even louder.

I don't know how long it is before I remember that it's Sunday. Dad planned it this way for a reason. There's no one coming to find me. Once again, he's abandoned me to my fate.

I'm dazed and in shock. While I scrunch my eyes closed, I'm morbidly drawn to opening them, unable to resist looking again and again at the bloody mess that was my father's body. I've never seen anyone deceased before. As a child, I was considered too young to view my mother after she'd passed.

Slowly, I realise while I've no idea what I should be doing, it has to be something. Putting out my hand, with the help of a chair, I get myself up on unsteady legs and begin to reach for the phone when my father's last words suddenly slam into me.

Money in the safe. Keys to a car.

My brow tightens, and my eyes crease as understanding washes over me. He planned it! He's given me a chance to escape and taken away the hold that Barclay had over me. Then, a more dire thought slams into my brain. Barclay now has no reason to keep me alive as his money cow is dead. If Dad's plan doesn't work, I'll be worse off than I've ever been.

What have you done, Dad? All I want to do is to be able to rewind the last few minutes.

Why didn't you talk to me? Why didn't you explain? Then I realise, taking his life wasn't something easy, and if he'd told me what he'd planned, I'd have tried to talk him out of it.

My father's made many mistakes. Not knowing how to parent and squandering money that brought us to where we are today. Not understanding how cruel a man like Barclay could be. But in the end, however misguided, he's made the ultimate sacrifice, and that's a debt I can never repay, especially if I squander the chance he's given to me. I've no option but to get away.

Snap decision made, I go to the safe which is ajar with the contents on show just as he'd said. I take out the money, more cash than I've ever seen in my life, and stuff it into my purse. Then I withdraw the keys, searching in vain for a note I hope my father had left for me, some last words of affection or wisdom to see me on my way, but there's nothing. He obviously had nothing more to say to me.

Surely I should hug my dad? Kiss him? I can't bring myself to go near him. Anything that made him the man that he was seems to have deserted his body. I resort to standing over him and telling him, despite his faults, that I've always loved him. Knowing I can't waste time, I force myself to turn and leave, unable to hope that it's not long before someone finds him and that whoever he is treats him with dignity.

My hand shakes as I press the button on the service elevator that takes me straight to the deserted underground parking lot. There's only one car other than my dad's there. A pang of sadness goes through me as I remember he'll never drive his again. Then, before I can break down, I click the fob, and the lights of the second car flash.

It's a Ford Explorer, not a recent model or flashy. One like a million others on the road. It makes me wonder how much time Dad had spent planning this, and boosts my resolve not to let him down. Everything he's done is wasted if Barclay finds me.

While time has seemed to slow, when I glance at my watch, only half an hour has passed since I entered the building. I probably have that much time again before my guards come searching for me. *No time to waste.*

I drive out of the parking garage and carefully exit onto the street, driving in the opposite direction to where my guards will be waiting. Following all the traffic laws so as to bring no attention, hands tightly gripping the steering wheel, I leave the city. I continue driving until the tank is nearly empty, top up, grab something to eat even though I don't feel hungry, and then take to the road again.

The more miles I can put between Barclay and me, the happier I will be.

Katrina Aster, née James, must completely disappear and never be seen again.

I'll do anything, absolutely anything, to ensure Barclay can never find me.

I won't waste Dad's legacy.

CHAPTER ONE
STRIDER

Placing a hard kick to his kidneys, I tell the man lying at my feet, "You're just fuckin' me off now. Tell me what you know about our missing product." His agonised yelp, blubbering and bloody face, even coupled with hands held up to ward me off, does nothing to bring forth any sympathy.

"Make it easy on yourself," my VP, Shotgun, growls from behind me.

"I… I… know nothing." The words are punctuated with sobs. "You've got to believe me," he cries. An acrid odour fills the air, and the darkening area around his crotch shows he's just pissed himself.

Oh for fuck's sake! I've had enough of this. Taking out my gun, I gift him with a bullet between the eyes. *There. Job done. Now I don't need to listen to his snivelling excuses anymore.*

The sounds of the shot are still echoing as Tequila shouts,

"What the fuck, Prez? We could have got decent intel out of him."

I raise my eyes and give him my best prez stare, the one that makes most men cower and shake in their boots. Unfortunately, it doesn't have that effect on my enforcer. And Buzz, my sergeant-at-arms, is looking equally unimpressed.

Shotgun regards me sadly and shakes his head. "Teq, call for Butch and Pete to come clean up this mess."

"Fuckin' prospects are going to get fed up with cleaning up after Prez soon," Buzz mumbles.

Lurching forward, I put my hand around his neck, forcing him back to the wall. "You got something you want to say to me?"

Emitting a heavy sigh, Shotgun steps between us, his hands resting on mine, loosening them to stop me from choking my sergeant-at-arms, who, loyal to the fucking bone, is doing nothing to defend himself. "Let's get out of here. We could all do with some wind therapy and definitely some fresh air." He glances at the body and wrinkles his nose.

I'm wound up, irate, angry with the world, with them, and especially with myself. What I just did was wrong. How are we ever going to find out who's dipping into our product if I fly off the handle and shoot any potential witnesses dead? I seem to have lost all the patience I ever had. Recently, when I look in the mirror, I don't recognise myself. Maybe the VP's right. A long ride might help clear my head. Trouble is, I'm not sure there are enough miles in the entire United States to achieve that result.

Letting Buzz go, ignoring him coughing and gasping in an effort to restore the air intake through his throat, I stomp toward the stairs and up out of the basement. At this time of day, the nightclub we run is empty of patrons, though there are a couple of cleaners getting things sorted out. Their proximity to my loss of control only moments ago makes me thank fuck that we've got a well-soundproofed location hidden away.

I leave via the rear entrance which leads to the parking lot where we left our bikes. Going to mine, I straddle it. Turning the key and pressing the start button, I'm tempted to just hit the road without waiting for anyone else. But even after my assault, Buzz would kill me if I tried to ride out alone, and Tequila would probably help him. The Wretched Soulz have too many enemies for a prez to be on his own on the road, so this time, from somewhere, I manage to tamp down my impatience.

Or at least until my men emerge from the basement. Once they're in my sight, I kick down into gear and rev the engine, releasing the clutch. As the bike leaps forward, the view in my mirror sends a brief grin to my face when I see my three offi-cers running to their bikes, throwing their legs over their machines, and starting their Harleys in unison.

Making no real effort to outrun them, they catch up with me before I join the freeway. Shotgun pulls up alongside me as I hit a red light.

"Where we going?" he asks, his voice loud enough to be heard over the even-while-idling-thundering Harley engine.

"Fuck knows," I yell back.

He shoots me a wide grin and slips back to ride alongside Buzz as the green glow gives us permission to proceed.

I hadn't lied. I've no fucking idea where I'm heading, but as the road opens up and I twist the throttle, the tension leaves my head and chest. Seemingly following some internal GPS, I take the route that finds me on Ranch Road 470 and drive through Bandera, which would, ironically, take me to the unlikely named Utopia were we to go that far. Doubtful it would fulfil its promise of bringing anything special into my life, I pull off at a spot where we can park up the bikes, only then realising we've been riding for almost two hours, and pleased I'd started off with a fully topped off tank.

Killing my engine, I slide my hand into my cut, take out a pack of cigarettes and light one.

Silence descends as the thundering of the bikes drawing up alongside me comes to a stop, to be replaced by the ticking of cooling engines.

Breathing out the long inhale of nicotine, I put my bike on its stand and get off, stretching with my hands on my hips, bending my back and rolling my shoulders, then shaking my head to get the kinks out of my neck. I release the tie holding my long hair and shrug it down my back.

"You done?" Shotgun comes up beside me.

As normal, a good ride has blown the cobwebs away. For a while, I'd been able to concentrate on nothing but the pavement beneath me and the clarity of air whooshing past me. It's as if the weight of my direst thoughts has been left back in the city. I smile as I grin back. "For now."

Buzz has manoeuvred so he's standing in front of me, his face turned toward the low hills that surround us, his hand shading his eyes from the sun. After he takes his bandanna and wipes sweat from his brow, he turns around and nods toward some rocks. "Seems like a good place to sit and have a talk."

The eagerness of my companions to show their agreement by immediately walking over and making themselves as comfortable as possible on their impromptu, unyielding seats has me narrowing my eyes.

What have we got to fuckin' talk about? We discuss anything necessary in church. Sure, right now it's just me and my top team, but I can think of no pressing business that can't be discussed in front of all the other members. Suspecting they're going to berate me for my display of temper, and unwilling to admit that they'd be right to do so, I stay where I am.

"Hey, come join us," Tequila calls out, indicating a rock in front of him.

"Rather get back on the road," I object.

Buzz fixes me with a stare. "Take a load off. It's a nice day."

"Yeah, when was the last time you just sat and relaxed?" Shotgun leans back on his elbows, stretches out his long legs and, closing his eyes, raises his face to the sun.

I can't remember the last time I allowed myself any downtime at all. Even sleep evades me most nights. Letting my mind drift means inviting the demons to speak up in my head. "There's time enough to relax when you're fuckin' dead." To make my point, I walk close enough to kick Shotgun's feet.

As if it's a signal, three men move at once, their calm state instantly gone. Instead of stress-free faces, their expressions are set. And, in their hands, guns have appeared.

I might have been an asshole over the last few months, but I've not done anything to damage the club. I can't consider for one moment that it's my patch or my life that they want. With a sigh and a shrug, holding my lit cigarette between two fingers and taking a last drag before stubbing it out beneath my boot, I take the hard seat they left for me.

"It's a fuckin' intervention," I surmise.

Shotgun grimaces. "I suppose you could call it that." He nods toward Buzz, who steps closer to me and curls his fingers in a gimme gesture.

"Don't make me take it from you," Buzz threatens.

I've gone head-to-head with Buzz before in the ring and know he's a more than competent fighter. Right now, I'd prefer to keep my ribs and jaw intact. Doesn't stop me from giving him a healthy glare as I surrender my gun. When that doesn't satisfy him, I also pass over my knife.

"Bit over the top isn't it?" I spit at Shotgun while Buzz parks his backside on his rocky perch again. When the VP shrugs, I narrow my gaze. "Don't worry, I'm happy with my revenge served cold."

He snorts at my threat. "Cold doesn't worry me. It's how hot-headed you've become that does. I'll take my chance of payback after we've had our say."

Tapping another cigarette out of my pack, I light up, breathing in deeply. Through the resultant exhale of blue smoke, I rasp, "So what's this a-fuckin'-bout?"

Tequila leans forward, putting his joined hands on his knees. "How are things going, Prez?" His voice is gentle, full of genuine concern.

These three men aren't just my most trusted brothers in the club. I've been riding with them for years. Long before I got my president's patch. They know everything about my life, all the parts I keep secret from everyone else—the shame, the sadness, the inevitability of a train wreck coming that I'm unable to stop. Rather than snapping, I say in a voice heavy with deep emotion, "Don't go there, Teq."

"You're a complicated fuckin' man, Brother," Shotgun starts. "For a while, I thought you were getting things balanced out." Confused, I raise an eyebrow, prompting him to continue. "No one... no one could blame you for going with Jasmine, but none of us can understand what's happening between you now. For the past few months, you've been like a bear with a sore paw, and your mood seems to correlate with the distance you're keeping from her."

Jasmine. I turn my head, refusing to look my brothers in the eye. She's the woman who haunts my nights, the one I can't get out of my mind. She's been intruding into places where she's no right to be, inside my head all the time.

"She's nothing to you anymore? That it?" Buzz asks. "She available now? 'Cause from where I'm sitting, we're supporting a club whore who doesn't work on her back."

"Or laps or any flat surface for that matter," Tequila interjects.

"You letting her loose, Bro? You going to let her open her legs to the rest of us?"

They might have disarmed me, but that doesn't stop me from flying at Shotgun, catching him by surprise and throwing him backward off his makeshift seat. I've got one heavy punch to his face when a bullet hits the ground far too close to my feet.

"Knock it off!" Buzz growls.

I stand back with my hands raised.

Ruefully rubbing his cheek and checking his nose is still firmly affixed to his face, Shotgun first gives a chin lift of thanks toward Buzz, and then states, "Guess that answers our question. Jasmine is still off-limits."

"Then we need to discuss what the hell she's doing in the club other than taking up space."

I spin around to Tequila but can't seem to do more than let my mouth open and shut. The words *she's mine* have to be swallowed down into my throat. She's not, and I can't think of the time when I hope that she would be, as that only acknowledges my upcoming loss.

"You haven't fucked her for months," Buzz observes.

Now that I can address. "You keeping a check on how often I get my dick wet?"

Buzz chortles. "Your mood says it all, Prez. As does hers."

The sun is beating down mercilessly, and their interrogation is making me sweat. I wipe moisture off with my bandanna. Then, in a monotone voice, I remind them, "She got pregnant." I brush a hand back through my hair, gathering it up and retying it into a ponytail. "She got fuckin' pregnant."

"And she sorted it." Shotgun's eyes narrow. "Is that what the problem is? She aborted your kid?"

It can't be. I'm the one who told her there was no way she could have my child. She did exactly what I wanted, and no one but me knew how much it hurt that she did. How my guilt was magnified as I knew how much she regretted it. "She got pregnant," I repeat, sticking to safe ground.

Buzz snorts his frustration. "Didn't think this was quite how this talk was going to go, Prez. But seems like you need to know some facts about the birds and bees. It takes two to tango. Jas didn't get in the family way all by herself."

She hadn't. I'd gloved up. Used a condom fresh from a pack. But still, she got pregnant. But for some reason, I can't stop blaming her more than myself.

Until then, I'd had a willing female partner to let me use her body whenever the urge took me. Hell, I'm no monk. I'm a red-blooded man who gets fed up with only using their hand. She'd offered me everything I needed—no emotions involved, just a joint physical need, itches that needed to be scratched.

Jasmine had walked into the club, a broken woman in need of a home. I'd seen her, taken her, monopolised her time. Pulling the prez card, they all knew she was mine. Not liking to share probably comes from me having grown up as an only child. There had been some murmuring but nothing serious. The brothers had enough other women to keep them satisfied.

Jasmine and I had had a good thing for over two years, both knowing the score and knowing there was never going to be anything real between us until it was interrupted a few months ago by those two little lines.

It was then it all went to shit.

"You know we're financing her project?"

Buzz's calmly spoken question takes a moment to compute in my head. *What project?* Since the fateful day, I've maintained distance from Jasmine, which is hard to do when we both spend most of our time in the club. But I go out of my way to avoid her. When she's out of sight, it's easier to try to keep her out of my mind. Now I'm starting to wonder what she's been getting up to and whether I should have kept a closer eye on her.

"What the fuck are you talking about?" I snap as I rack my brain. "I don't remember authorising giving her money."

"We don't give her any more than we do the other club pussy," Shotgun points out. "Lodging and food for a start. And the pocket money so they can buy the shit they need."

"I ask again," my voice a deep growl, "what the fuck are you talking about? In what way are we financing her, and what fuckin' project?"

Tequila narrows his eyes as he glances my way. "We provide food and keep to a woman who doesn't work as a club girl. It's left her with time on her hands. You truly never see what she's up to when she's in the clubroom? When she has that laptop open all the time?"

I might try to avoid looking at her, though I'm always overly aware of her presence when she's in my proximity, the sense of her being close, that unique perfume that seems to surround her. I don't let my gaze linger even when she catches my eye. My temptation, my guilt, making me keep my distance.

I tap out another cigarette as I try to imagine what they all know that I don't. One answer comes to mind. "She running an online business or something?" Jasmine is smart. I know nothing about her level of education, but one of my most poignant memories of her is lying in bed after sex and just talking. Her natural intelligence, her unique insight on things, I'd enjoyed our conversations. But remembering isn't doing me any good. *I can't have her.*

"Well, it's something, all right." Tequila laughs as Buzz gets up, goes to his saddlebags and returns carrying an object.

When he hands it to me, I take it and see it's a paperback book. I glance at the title, *Falling for the Club President,* and then at the author name, *J. Frobisher.* Neither tells me a lot. I flick through the pages and words leap out that let me know it's a romance novel, the type of book I've seen Jasmine read before. *Motorcycle club romance.* Fuck, a glorified, sanitised view of life with bikers. I remember teasing her about it. Disinterested, I start to hand the book back.

Shaking his head, Buzz refuses to take it from me. "There's more. *Falling for the Club Enforcer, Falling for the Sergeant-at-Arms, and Falling for the Road Captain.*"

"So?" Are they going to tell me they've caught Jasmine reading books? For fuck's sake, where's the crime in that? She's free to do whatever she wants with the little money she gets from the club. "Jas reads. I already knew that."

Shotgun barks a laugh. "Not these," he remarks, then frowns. "Well, I suppose she has to. But these particular books? Well, these are the ones she writes."

She writes?

I tap on the cover. "Say's it's written by a woman, or man, called Frobisher. Jasmine's surname is Smart."

Buzz sighs. "Ever heard of pen names, Prez? Apparently, Frobisher was the maiden name of a grandmother she had fond feelings for."

My eyes open wide that the author really is her. Jasmine has written a book. Several of them, by the sound of it. An unexpected wave of pride washes over me. I always knew she had a spark. "You've read them?"

I suppose I've addressed my question to them all, but don't expect them all to nod.

"Had to," Shotgun states. "Wanted to make sure it was all fiction. Don't want her giving away secrets about the club."

"And they're fuckin' good!" Tequila remarks. "Good writing for a chick. Full of adventure and suspense."

"And sex," Buzz drops in. "Don't forget the sex."

Shotgun snorts. "Can't forget that."

I glare at them all. Having forgotten my lit cigarette, it's dripping with ash. I tap it off, and then take a long drag. The wheels in my brain start to turn. "Jasmine's making an income from this?" Buzz's nod and accompanying shrug suggest he thinks so but doesn't know. I breathe deep, then let out a breath. "You want me to cut her loose from the club? You think that's going to make me feel better?"

It's an answer, I suppose. Out of sight, out of mind. Wouldn't need to feel guilty if she's found a way of supporting herself. My stomach grips tight as though I've eaten something I'm allergic to. *Let her go?* It would be for the best...

"Fuck no," Shotgun barks. "That book," he nods at the one in my hand, "is the latest she's published. Think you better read it, Prez."

Read it? I'm no reader. Well, not unless it's a Harley manual or some such. I start to shake my head but notice the intense look in my VP's eyes.

"There's something in here I'm not going to be happy about, isn't there?" My brain automatically goes to the place where Jasmine has unwittingly betrayed us. Maybe disclosed some innermost workings of the club to our enemies. And if so, how much repair work will I have to do, and am I going to have to punish her?

Betrayers of the club end up six feet under.

Hesitantly, I glance at the book, and then my gaze lands on my VP, my sergeant-at-arms, and my enforcer in turn. I swallow hard, then speak when I'm sure there's no unsteadiness in my voice. "This is serious, isn't it?"

"As fuck," Shotgun answers.

CHAPTER TWO

JASMINE

SIX MONTHS AGO...

Noting the caller display on my phone, I'm already smiling as I place one hip on my bed, curling up the other leg beside me. "Hey, girl. It's so good to hear from you."

"Are you sure?" a tentative voice speaks into my ear.

"Fuck, yeah." I chuckle. I'd met Sheri eight months back when she and her man, StoryTeller, had sought refuge at the Wretched Soulz Texas Charter's clubhouse. It had been an explosive entrance, coming in hot through the gates with a rogue member of the Dominators MC after them. Sheri was lucky to be alive. A bullet had hit her backpack, embedding itself in the very book that had brought her and StoryTeller together. Remembering, I sigh, a romantic story, but one for another day. I'd quickly discovered that she'd been carrying precious cargo, and when that news was known, doubly glad she'd be okay. "How's the babe?"

A wail in the background announces that little Maria isn't

far away. "Grumpy." Sheri laughs. "She always seems to know when I want a moment to myself. You got her, Jake?" The last three words were a bit muffled, as if she'd turned her head away, so I'm not surprised when I hear StoryTeller's voice give a confirmatory response, and then the crying fades away. "Jake's so good with her," Sheri confides. "A real doting dad."

She hadn't expected it would turn out that way. Her pregnancy shocked them both, which is how Sheri knows so much of my life. I'd been in the position of being able to facilitate her choice if she'd wanted things to go the other way. I'd been in the same position a short while before and why she was reticent about making contact today. I know what a surprise pregnancy is like, only mine didn't have a happy ending. Encouraged to do the "right" thing by the dad, I'd taken the tablets and regretted I had the very next day.

Life's a bitch, isn't it? Strider had been so adamant he wasn't ready to be a father, so I'd done what he wanted. Only, pretty soon, I had doubts. He's never been the same with me since, and I don't know why. Our casual sexual relationship had become tense. Strider found excuses to keep his distance until the point came when I couldn't remember when I last warmed his bed.

Does he blame me for getting pregnant when the condom broke? Or, even with me now on the pill and him still gloving up, does he not want to run the same risk? Or, worse, does he regret the life that could have been and which he pressured me to throw away? Whatever, he and I have never gotten back to the easy relationship we once had.

Not that I have any claim on him. Technically, I'm a club girl, theoretically available to all the men. But Strider had made it known I was only there for him. Even now, when it's been weeks since he's asked me to meet his needs, I'm still left alone by the brothers. I've naturally fallen into being a sort of house mom—tending bar, looking after the clubhouse, and making sure the other girls stay in line.

"So, what's it like being a mom?" I ask Sheri, pulling my thoughts away from comparisons between her man and mine.

"Hard work." She laughs. "I thought babies were supposed to sleep all the time. I fast found out that's a lie. But enough about me. I rang to see how you were. Tell me something that doesn't involve talking about expressing milk or diapers."

I snort. "But you're loving it, aren't you?" I don't need to wait for her reply. I hear it in her laugh. Obliging her, I move to a different topic and prepare to tell her my news. After taking a deep breath, I leap off the cliff and confide, "I've written a book."

There's silence at the end of the line, then I hear the air leave her lungs in a whoosh. "A *book*? Oh my God, Jas. That's amazing. What's it about?"

Unable to suppress the grin on my face, I lean back against the pillow. "It's an MC romance, of course."

"That's amazing. It will be brilliant." Her words tumble out one after another and I appreciate the confidence she has. "You live the life. It's got to be great. Is it published yet?"

After futilely shaking my head, I say the words, "No. I'm kinda embarrassed, you know? I don't know if it's good enough. Before I launch it into the world, I probably need to get it properly edited and proofread. I've no clue how to do that."

"Have you got a cover?"

I've got nothing. Just a ton of words written in a document. "Not yet."

There's a pause before she asks hesitantly, "Would you let me read it?"

Breathing out heavily, it's been something I've thought about, and partly why I'm so grateful to hear from her. I confirm, "I'd love that. I'm nervous, of course, but you know the genre. I'd like your honest opinion on whether I'm on the right track." I know she loves the same books as I do, as she'd attended the Motorcycle, Mobsters and Mayhem signing, where she'd picked up the book that ended up saving her life.

"Send it to me," she demands. "I really can't wait."

We spend a couple of moments exchanging pleasantries, then end the call. Before I can have second thoughts, I send the promised email and attachment.

I then try and forget that someone else will be reading my words, expecting it to be an agonising few weeks before I receive any comment from her, and certainly don't anticipate getting positive feedback. In my head, my story makes sense. I cried, laughed and raged while I was writing it. But I have no idea if I translated the images in my mind sufficiently well to the written word. Was my language too simple, my grammar incorrect, the sentences awkward, too long, too short? Was my manuscript going to be a disaster in a myriad of any possible ways? My education had focused on being academic, not creative writing. Who the hell am I to believe I could write a book? Or, at least, one other people would want to read.

Despite my fears about my first book's reception, those voices, now having found an audience, just keep speaking in my head. Deciding even if I'm the only person ever to read my stories, I won't stop. I'm finding it's as much fun writing books as I have reading them.

It would be amazing if I could actually make some money doing this. Part of me is terrified that I'll soon be wearing out my welcome with the Wretched Soulz MC.

When I first arrived at the clubhouse looking for sanctuary, I'd made up my mind I'd do anything I had to, just to have their powerful protection on my side. I'd rationalised that I'd become accustomed to being raped before, so what would it matter if I had to let any of the men in the club use my body? The difference would be that it would be with my consent this time. With no other option, I considered it a necessary evil to keep me safe. I knew motorcycle clubs looked after their property. Paying for the privilege of shelter and security with my god-given assets wasn't too great a price. Nothing they could do could be worse than my previous experience.

Had I been scared? Of course, I had. I'd no idea what I was getting myself into. I'd had to steady my nerves with Dutch courage before I was brave enough to put a swing in my step and walk into the room full of leather-clad men. I'd worn a tight cropped tee that showed off my tits and a short tight skirt which would leave nothing to the imagination if I bent over. High heels made the most of my shapely calves and long legs. My hair gleamed and fell in tight curls around my shoulders. My eyes were smouldering due to the makeup I'd applied, and I had full, red-painted lips.

I nearly changed my mind and ran when it seemed like everyone had turned to look at me, but before I had a chance, something caught my eye. Or rather, someone.

A man standing in the middle of a group in front of a bar, charismatic, tall, and so damn muscular, his arms seemed like they were bursting from his cut. His hair, tumbling down, framed spectacular chiselled features. My body hadn't been aroused by sex for three long years, yet as his dark eyes seemed to blaze into mine, butterflies swirled in my stomach, and, embarrassingly in this short skirt, my panties felt decidedly wet.

As he approached, he raised an eyebrow, and his mouth was curved into a slight smirk. He didn't make any introduction or small talk. He just grabbed hold of my hand and, with gentle persuasion, tugged me in the way he wanted to go, which was straight through the rowdy clubroom, out the back to the room where he stayed.

It was there that I realised he wore the patch that denoted he was the *President*. And there that he brought my body back to life. Even now, just thinking about it, my thighs clench together in an effort to ease the ache. His body was proportionate and well-endowed, and he knew how to use what the deities had given him. It wasn't a quick fuck, well, it was at first, I suppose, and then he took his time. He worshipped my body as if he were an attentive lover rather than a biker using a whore.

When we'd finished, I thought he was going to kick me out of bed, but instead, his arm curled around me, pulling me into his side.

His words, gruffly spoken, informed me, "This is all I'm offering. There ain't gonna be no happy ending, no old lady patch or title. You're a club girl, club property, but while we've got this spark between us, you'll be exclusively mine." He'd chuckled softly. "Don't want the brothers dipping into your honey pot."

I remember sleeping more peacefully that night than I'd done for a very long time. Strider, as I came to know him, wasn't going to be a permanent fixture in my life. I knew it was only a matter of time. Maybe just a few days, weeks, or months if I was lucky, but I needed this breathing space.

And, well, wow. That man was just fine.

But the end date never appeared on the horizon, and I settled into my new life. The teasing of the brothers about him not sharing his toys soon faded, and they accepted my odd position in the club. I was his, but I wasn't. And discombobulated from all the rapid changes I'd been through—my forced marriage, the abuse my husband had put me through, then witnessing the death of my father had left my mind in a whirl.

This strange situation with no pressures or expectations was exactly what I needed.

Strider was a generous lover, making sex fun, and quite happy to snuggle and relax afterward. Until he wasn't.

Now, he rarely comes for me anymore. I don't just miss the physical gratification but feel I've lost a friend.

It wasn't like a switch being thrown. After I ended the pregnancy, for a month or so, things seemed to go back to normal, but in hindsight, I was only kidding myself. At first, I thought Strider was holding back as he didn't want to hurt me, but then I realised he was backing away emotionally as well as physically. When days became weeks and weeks turned into months, I knew he was finished with me, though no words to that ilk had been exchanged.

It was then that I wondered whether I was going to have to throw my hat into the pool of club whores.

It wasn't anything different from my original expectations two years back, I reminded myself. And my need for a secure base with men who'd protect me hadn't changed. Mentally, though, I'd not only enjoyed being just one man's plaything, and stupid of me, while I hadn't realised I was doing it, I'd fallen in love.

Going with someone else would feel like betrayal.

But it had never happened. No one asked me to put out, even though they could all see Strider no longer wanted anything to do with me. It was as if I was still somehow branded as his.

Then, as now, I feel like a fraud, here under false pretences. I make myself useful—cleaning around the club, cooking, and stepping into catfights between the other girls. But even I'm not fooling myself. It's nothing worth what they're giving to me—security and protection, a place to hide. I've no idea how long it's going to last.

For the present, I'll make the most of it. And, while it's probably stupid, I'm pinning all my hopes on being able to write books.

Having sent my first draft to Sheri, I can't relax. My finger-nails are bitten down to the quick. Despite building up my expectation to be disappointed, I can't help but hope she finds at least some merit in it. Something I can build on, perhaps.

It's less than twenty-four hours after I sent her the email, when my phone trills again, and it's her calling me back.

"Oh my God," I breathe. "Is it that bad? You couldn't finish it?"

"Couldn't finish it?" She snorts down the line. "Hell, girl, I finished it. I've never read a book so fast. Ask Jake. I stayed up all night as I couldn't put it down. It's freaking fantastic."

I shake my head as if to clear my ears. "Wh-what?"

"It's amazing. Best book I've read in ages. I want more."

It's taking me a few seconds to process her words. *Is she just being kind?* "Do you really mean that?"

"Of course I do." She chuckles down the line. "The story is amazing. The plot draws you in, and everything's so realistic to this life."

I can't believe what I'm hearing. I didn't even dare dream of a reaction like that. "You didn't find anything wrong?"

"Well, sure, there were a lot of typos and a few words I think you got wrong. But that's nothing a good editor can't fix."

Where the hell do I find an editor? I don't ask that question aloud as another is more important. "How could I afford someone like that, Sheri? Those professionals would cost thousands."

"Er," she starts, hesitantly. "I've got some ideas if you don't mind giving me a few days to see if I can get some help for you?"

"Honey, I'd give you a year if you thought it would help." Internally, I feel a buzz of excitement begin to grow. Sheri, a woman I admire and who shares my love of the MC genre, actually likes my book. Actually, she thinks it could be published.

"I'll be in touch," she tells me. "Take care of yourself."

"Take care of you," I respond automatically.

As it turned out, though, it was she who took care of me. God knows how she found time with a baby, but she joined Facebook groups, became friendly with PAs and authors, and found me an editor whom I could afford. Having read the book, she knew my description of the hero and looked through all the stock photo sites to find a cheap photo that matched him to a T. And then, somehow, she found a cover designer.

Before I knew it, I had a formatter, and a book that I could load up and send off into the big bad world. I swear I felt as nervous as any mother bidding farewell to their firstborn on the first day at school.

Book one wasn't a bestseller or anything like that, but the sales and reviews were enough to encourage me. Once I'd started writing, I found it addictive and hard to stop, so more books flowed. As each added to the series, I started to make a few bucks. And hey, to my amazement, I soon found I was turning a profit.

I owe so much to Sheri. I swear she knows my books better than I know them myself and always points out inconsistencies between the stories.

Fast forward six months, and I've just published my third book.

Even more exciting, Sheri encouraged me to get on the waitlist for the next Motorcycle, Mobsters and Mayhem signing, and I've just received an invite.

Me. *What the fuck?*

When I first met Sheri, I was jealous she'd been to the signing that I'd have liked to have gone to myself. As a reader, of course. And now? Now I'm going to be attending as a freaking bonafide author!

Sure, there are a few ways life could be better. But this? Abused wife to club whore to author? There's surely little that could be better than that.

Nowadays, Sheri and I communicate by sending messages, so a phone call takes me by surprise. I answer with a twin sense of anticipation and dread as I've just sent her the first draft of my fourth book.

Instead of answering with a polite "hello", I dive straight in. "Is it dreadful?"

"Fuck, no." She laughs. "But..."

"But?" I prompt when the silence stretches out.

"Oh, Jas. You broke my heart with that book. It's you and Strider, isn't it? Or, at least, the way you hoped it would have worked out."

I swallow hard, and my voice is as low as a whisper. "Have I really been so obvious?"

She doesn't reply for a moment. "I only made the connection because I know you. It won't be to anyone else. Since no one in the club is going to read your book, there'll be no one who'll suss it out. It's an amazing story—bittersweet, so suspenseful, so many ups and downs and then a happy ending. You really have an amazing imagination."

Yeah. I have an imagination, all right. Maybe the problem is that I didn't rely on it too much when I wrote this particular book. But as Sheri says, no one who actually knows me will read it.

My secrets are safe.

And so is my foolish admission that I fell in love with Strider.

CHAPTER THREE
STRIDER

Flanked by Shotgun and followed by the sergeant-at-arms and enforcer, I head directly back to the club. I'm riding by instinct, barely conscious of the road disappearing beneath my wheels. My emotions are all over the place.

Another man might want to shoot the balls off any men who'd organised such an intervention, but the VP, Buzz, and Tequila are not only my brothers-in-arms, but my best friends. They've been in my life for as long as I can remember. Initially annoyed, I'd quickly realised they wouldn't have said anything had I not let things, and myself, get out of control. And for that, the person I'm most angry with is me. I wouldn't have been made prez if I wasn't levelheaded in all situations, especially those where the outcome could be that men would live or die. The last few months, though, my temper's been short, my patience non-existent.

I'm embarrassed that they've identified something I'd refused to admit to myself, that my problems all harp back to my personal life, which should never have been allowed to fall back onto the club. Hell, I managed to keep it separate for years until Jasmine, who was only supposed to be a pleasant diversion in the sack. *But she'd crept under my skin,* and I couldn't handle it. When, well, when she, no, *we,* my brothers are right, had made that mistake, inside, I was falling to pieces, and my exasperation with myself affected my performance in the club.

Now, I've another sentiment to contend with. *Fear.* At first, I was surprised but delighted for Jasmine that she'd been writing books. Good for her. I always knew she was too clever to bury herself in a life as a club girl. But my officers would never have brought it to my attention if it was only that she'd been working for herself on the club's dime—she does enough for us, tending bar and keeping the other whores in line. But having been around the club for three years, she won't have been blind to some of the more shady things that have gone down. Some of which might make excellent material for a novel. *Fuck it.* Did she know too much? Has she stepped over the line?

What do I do if she has? If she was a man telling tales on us, she'd pay with her life. If she's committed a crime, I'm the prez, and I can't be weak if punishment needs to be meted out.

How bad could it be? Could she draw the attention of law enforcement to us or have given away secrets that our enemies would love? Has she talked about our armaments, strengths or weaknesses? For Shotgun, Buzz, and Tequila to be concerned, it has to be serious.

Still, on autopilot, I ride through the gate that the prospect has opened and back into my parking spot. With just a raise of my chin, I leave my companions, walk through the clubhouse, grabbing a bottle of Jack from the bar, and continue on out back to the motel-like setup that houses our rooms. I offer some curt response when brothers greet me. My single focus is on getting some privacy so I can start to read.

As I've a house off compound that I tend to stay in most nights, and a life outside the club, my room here is just like that of my brothers'—a place to lay my head and not much else. Unlocking the door, I step inside, taking off my boots and slinging my cut casually over the back of a chair, grateful my brothers can't see the disrespect I show to it. Right now, I'm too worried to care. I take the book I'd been given out of my pocket, regarding it like a venomous snake that could strike me at any moment.

It seems innocuous enough. A tattooed, bare-chested man on the cover, the author's name, *J Frobisher,* under the title.

Twisting the cap off the bottle, I take a long swig, then settle myself on the bed. As I flick to the first page, I wince at the number of words, unable to remember the last time I read anything that wasn't a bike spec, nor something without text being broken up by pictures. *Damn, it's going to be a long night.* Then, with a deep sigh, I turn to the first page. *What the fuck has she written that's got my officers' balls in a twist?*

I bark a laugh. Hell, I didn't expect that. From the first paragraph, I'm drawn into a picture of a motorcycle club, that, yeah, could be similar to ours, but it's not. This is the fourth book in the series, and it seems a number of brothers have already been caught in the old lady trap. But not the prez. And hell, I can relate to that.

There are even cute babies being born and kids hanging around. I suppose I could see why someone might be worried about that, but I can't think Jasmine's writing is going to infect the club. Oh, I bark a laugh when I see one of the brothers works at a crematorium—and hell, why didn't I think of that? Great way of body disposal. *Maybe I should ask Jasmine for advice about running my club.* Turning onto my back, I hold the book above me, take another sip of Jack, and find I'm really enjoying myself.

She's talented as fuck. Her words just roll off the page. It's so easy to read, simplistic language perhaps, but in a manner that I can relate to. Instead of being bored, of forcing myself to read on, I find myself turning page after page thrilled to see what comes next. *Uh-uh. Fuck, what an asshole.* I start to read about the hero, or anti-hero perhaps. He's the president of the club, and if I were to meet him in real life, I'd call him a dick.

He treats the main girl in the story like shit. *How does she put up with him?* But as I turn the pages faster, my attention caught, I read about how opposites attract, about how from the first moment he'd met her, the prez wanted no other woman. But rather than admit how smitten he was, he convinced himself, her, and everyone around him that all he wanted was sex. Of course, while insisting she be only his...

Hang on.

Rolling over onto one elbow, I take another mouthful of Jack, which seems to sour as soon as it hits my stomach. *No wonder they told me to read this.*

The gist of the story is the unrequited love of the club girl toward the prez, and how she lived for his scant praise and compliments. At first, it could read like she was belittling herself, but she's clearly the more intelligent one in the relationship, recognising it for what it is. Reading between the lines and knowing how much he wants her, even though he doesn't want to admit it.

The sex between them is off-the-charts hot, as if he's using his body to tell her what his mind cannot. I try to skim over the details but am soon dragged in. As I read how he pleases her, my hand reaches down, undoes my zipper and frees my dick. Hell, the words transport me back in time, and my mind conjures up Jasmine's hands on me. I read on, but now it's not the fictional characters having their fun. All I can picture is Jas as she takes my cock in her mouth. She uses suction, drawing me deep, then releasing me, her hands stroking what she can't take in. Her teeth rasp gently. She brings me almost to the peak, then backs off. Lifting briefly away, her knowing grin lights her face until she goes in for the kill—or the *petite mort*, the little death, and I've no chance to stop the eruption that floods from my dick and soaks the sheets.

My breathing is heavy, my lungs starved for air. *Only her. Only Jasmine.* No one else has brought me to such a peak. And, it seems, she doesn't even need to be present in my room to make me see stars.

Closing my eyes, I try to get the real life woman out of my mind and go back to the book. Telling myself firmly this is not about me and her. This is fiction. It's all made up in her mind.

I read on, hating how the prez is pulling away when all he ever wants is right there in front of his eyes. How he denies his emotions until... Until, he's forced to own up to his feelings when the condom splits.

A pregnancy scare.

I stop reading. Memories flood into my mind as I go back in time to that fateful morning.

"I'm pregnant."

I'm stunned. Lost for words. Then only one thing comes to me. *"You can't be."*

It's impossible for me to miss the hope in Jasmine's eyes. The optimism that I'll be okay with the predicament she's putting me in. But there is no way she can understand.

Becoming pregnant takes two. I gloved up and used my own condoms. Despite that, for some reason, my brain screams it's all her fault. This can't be happening. Not now, not with her. It's the worst possible time.

The solution is obvious. "Get rid of it."

I don't bother to discuss it with her or ask for her opinion. Making it an easy process, I used my connections and got the tablets that would solve the problem fast. Ignoring her obvious distress, I trust her when she agrees to take the medication. I can't explain how I can't do anything else or consider any other alternative. To let her carry my child is too big a betrayal.

Only a few days later and she confirms, "It's done."

From that fateful moment, I knew something inside Jasmine had died. Though she tried to hide her grief, I know she was shattered. I couldn't even comfort her as I wasn't able to turn back time.

I'd had no choice.

My eyes are leaking, and I angrily wipe the moisture away. I couldn't have done anything different. I made the only decision I could at the time. I can barely bring myself to keep reading, but I submit to my torture as in Jasmine's fictional world, the prez steps up, comes to his senses in ways I never have, and declares his undying love for the club girl. Eight months later, they welcome a beautiful baby girl.

I slam the book closed even though I've only read halfway.

Could that have been us? There's no doubt in my mind that while the characters' names are different, and the club bears no relation to the Wretched Soulz, that she's been writing the story that she wished could have been hers in real life.

I've never explained to her my reasons. And worse, my own guilt at my actions made me keep my distance, so both of us dealt with our loss on our own.

My gut clenches as I admit how much I hurt her. Unable to bear seeing the grief at my own loss mirrored in her eyes, and knowing I was the cause of it, kept me away. It was easier not to talk to her than face up to what I'd done. I'd tried to justify my behaviour to myself—*she's just a club girl. She knows the score. No strings, no attachments.*

The truth was my own feelings ran deep for her, emotions I couldn't allow. Having never asked her, I told myself that what I felt was one-sided. It was different for her.

Me? I knew I could cope with things I couldn't have. I'd been doing that for a very long time. But Jasmine? Well, she would be fine.

I'd been both wrong and blind. This book? I can feel her in every word, every sentence, every page. *This* is the longing deep from her heart. *This* is the ending she wanted. The prez and the club girl making a new start.

Eventually, the combination of the Jack I've consumed and my emotional turmoil has me passing out. Surprisingly, I wake with my mind full of clarity and a decision about a course of action I've not considered before.

While there are reasons things between us can never be as apparently we both wish they could, at least I can give Jasmine an explanation as to why. She deserves that, at least.

CHAPTER FOUR
JASMINE

"Hey, Butch. Watch out," I shout.

The prospect jumps, heeds my warning, and gets the near-burning bacon off the heat. He gives a wide grin in response to my rolling eyes. Sometimes, I think I'd prefer to do all the kitchen duties myself. Supervising can give me hives.

"This enough eggs?" Kat, the club girl who's been here the longest, asks in her lazy drawl.

Leaning over to check, I respond, "Sure, honey. That's more than enough."

"Impossible!" Shout laughs, entering the room and having overheard. "We'll eat everything you serve up."

"Ain't that the truth." Kat winks at me.

Laughing, I go check that the coffee pot doesn't need a refill, and finding it does, am just about to undertake that task when loud stomping footsteps approach.

"You. With me," is barked out.

We all swing around but it's me who Strider is clearly pointing to.

Brushing my hands down my jeans, I hate the way my heart rate speeds up. Nowadays, any attention from Strider is so unusual I can't be unaffected. But it's immediately apparent this is no request for a booty call. *Have I fucked up?*

Swallowing rapidly, I nod. "Sure, Prez. How can I help?"

Deigning not to answer, he simply stands back in silent invitation for me to precede him out of the door. Then he places his hand on my lower back to guide me. His touch burns, resonating through to my soul. *I've missed him so much.* I swallow hard, trying to stop feelings I shouldn't have from overwhelming me. *He's not mine. He'll never be.* As far as I know, he's about to chuck me out of the club.

The feeling he's had enough of me intensifies when I realise he's pushing me toward the front door. I wait for him to stop, to say some form of the words, "get out", but nothing comes from his mouth.

Once through the portal, he pauses, half-turns toward his bike, then lets a long breath out. Changing direction, he heads to one of the club's SUVs and opens the passenger door.

All my stuff is back inside in the small room I'd had assigned to me. Everything I possess in life, and, crucially, my laptop. Without that, I can't work. Rather than simply obey him, I put one hand against the side of the car and push back.

"Not like this, Strider." Again, I swallow hard. "You want me to leave? I'll give you no problem. But at least let me go pack first." Unless... A little voice says maybe he thinks I've learned too much about the club. If so, there's no way he can leave me alive.

Is this it? Is he going to kill me?

"Fuck, Jas. What are you thinking? You've gone white." Taking his hands off me, Strider takes a step back. "I'm not kicking you out. I've just got something I need to show you."

I've spent three years of my life loving this man, but love is not totally blind. I know it's one-sided. And when the emotion isn't reciprocated, trust and love don't go hand in hand. If Strider wants to get rid of me, he'll make some excuse to get me into the car.

Strider's a big man, and while my eyes flick left and right, he's still standing too close for me to try to get past him. Stronger than me, there's no way I'd be able to push him out of my path.

"Jas," he says in an imploring tone. "Please don't make this hard."

What? If he's going to take me somewhere to kill me and dispose of my body, why should I make it less difficult? I shake my head.

Reaching out his hand, he touches my shoulder, frowning as I visibly flinch. "What the fuck, Jas?" His eyes narrow more. "Where the hell do you think I'm taking you?"

Again, moving my head from side to side, I keep quiet. It seems stupid to voice my fears. I've never been afraid of Strider since the day that we met. In awe, yes, and respectful of his rank. But I've never been scared of him hurting me. Not until now, when he's acting so out of character.

"Talk to me, Jas."

Swallowing hard and licking my lips, I at last find some words. "You haven't wanted to be near me for weeks, months, Strider. Now, suddenly, out of the blue, you've something to show me?"

"I'm fuckin' this up," he says under his breath, causing me to strain to hear. His hand, still on my shoulder, gives a gentle squeeze. "I read your last book."

I catch a breath as my eyes open wide. Never in all the time I've known Strider have I ever seen him with anything other than a parts magazine or a bike manual. He's never once opened a book in my presence.

I don't need to say anything. He can see the doubt written on my face.

"Buzz said I should." He gives a half-hearted shrug.

"You read it all?" I query, my stomach dropping, hoping he might just have flicked through a couple of pages. I wonder whether there's any chance I could convince him it's all made up.

He disavows me of that. "I read enough." His Adam's apple moves in his throat. "Fuck, Jas. I didn't realise the feelings you had for me." His eyes search mine, and I try and turn away, but with his free hand, he grabs my chin and moves me to face him again. "Am I wrong? In your book, the club girl fell for the prez."

She had. Just like I had done. I'd set out the outcome I wished there could have been.

He can see it written on my face as he adds in a sad, gruff tone, "You were writing about me and you, weren't you?"

I let my lids shutter my eyes, not wanting him to be able to read my thoughts. It would be easier to tell him that his assumptions are incorrect and that I wasn't writing about any particular person. But I can't tell a lie. As the story came into my head, it was impossible to stop the words from flowing. The characters did what they wanted to do, and I knew it was my inner dreams talking. While I never told him I love him, it doesn't make it any less true.

When he pulls me to him, I allow myself to relax into his arms. It's been a while since he's held me, and selfishly, I breathe in the scent of that sandalwood shower gel he always uses mingled with leather and oil. It's so familiar, for a moment, I don't care what he does to me, as long as he keeps holding me.

"Jas," he murmurs softly into my ear. "I never wanted to hurt you. I thought we could just fuck, no emotions involved.

But it didn't turn out like that. I didn't want anyone else to touch you, but..." he pauses, swallows, then adds, "I couldn't make you mine." He pulls back slowly, almost reluctantly, and while I lose the warmth of his body, his hands cradle my face. "I shouldn't have gotten close to you, and I should have explained. Now, I want to show you why I have nothing to offer you." Leaning forward, he rests his lips against mine for a moment. "Can't blame you for not trusting me, but please, please, Jas. Come with me now."

What else can I say? Knowing he's never knowingly hurt me and trusting he won't start now, I reply with just one word, "Yes." Maybe if I understand the reasons for his actions, it will make his rejection ache less.

This time, when he opens the door, I get in. He reaches over me to pull the seat belt across and tightens it. Then he moves around to the driver's side.

He pulls out of the compound, not offering the exact location we're going, and I'm too nervous to ask. I rack my brains but can't come up with any explanation or suggestion of what he might want to show me. And as we drive, I can't bring myself to ask.

It's not a great distance until we're going through a nicely kept residential area, two-storey houses to either side with nice gardens and distance between them. If I'm honest, the type of place I've dreamed of living in. Not as ostentatious as where I grew up, but somewhere with a cosy, homely vibe. He pulls into a driveway and puts the car in park.

I eye the building in front of me—nicely maintained, and a decent front yard. When he makes no move to get out of the car, I ask, "Where are we?"

"At my house." He sounds curt.

I already knew he had a place away from the club. He's got a room there but rarely uses it to sleep, especially nowadays when I'm no longer warming his bed. "Okay," I respond slowly. "But why am I here?"

A quick glance toward him shows me his jaw is clenched. A moment passes, then two, before he explains, "I've brought you to meet my wife."

His wife? Now hold on one hot damn moment. Turning away from him, I focus my eyes on the front of the house. The fact he's married doesn't surprise me. Many bikers live a double life. That no one in the club ever mentioned he had a serious other half doesn't confound me either. The bro code trumps all. I just, never for one second, had even considered Strider had a permanent woman in his life.

I've been so fucking stupid. Those tender touches, the hours spent just talking. Those many times he kept me in his bed, wanting me to stay the night, had me thinking I was something special to him when, all it turns out I am, was the woman on the side. I, of all people, knowing how cruel men could be, would never have knowingly put myself in this position.

My fingers curl into my palms as I think through the implications. I was never anything more than a pleasant distraction on those nights he did stay at the club. It's no wonder he didn't want a baby with me. I'm angry at him, but more so at myself. Surely, I should have been able to recognise the signs? But Strider never smelled of perfume. There was no clue to destroy the fantasy I'd built up in my mind that he was mine.

When coming to the club, I had no good expectations about the men I would find, my sole purpose being to place myself under their protection. So why should I be shocked now when I find the president, himself, is a philandering bastard? I shouldn't be surprised.

What I can't understand is why he's brought me here now? Is it to punish me for clearly developing thoughts I should never have about him? *Does she know about me, or is he going to flaunt me in her face?* Did my story about the successful love affair between the president and the club girl make him think he needed to leave me in no doubt that he's already taken?

He's so wrong if he thinks I'll try to sink my claws into him. He's not been near me in months, and if that wasn't a damn red flag that he's not interested, I don't know what it would take. I certainly don't need any further introduction into his domestic life to steer clear of him. Hasn't he already hurt me enough?

"Take me back to the club," I spit out.

"No." He doesn't even spare me a glance as he refuses.

Incensed, I let my voice rise. "Not up for negotiation. You've made your point. I don't need a screaming match with your *wife* to confirm that you're off the market."

Now he turns to face me, his eyes wide. "That's not—"

I slam my fist into my palm, half wishing I was hitting the face of the obstinate man. "Strider! We had fun. Sure, I might have had some feelings for you, but you've made your point. Take me back."

"Just get out of the fuckin' car," he growls.

I'm going to get out of the car, alright. I'm going to be calling myself an Uber and heading back to the club. He's playing some game, and I want no part of it. Pushing hard, the door flies open and I all but stumble out.

But my escape plan is quickly foiled as he's moved fast. He catches me before I've even rounded the back of the car, takes me by the arm, and turns me around. While not a painful hold, it's enough that I can't get loose.

"For fuck's sake, Strider..."

He stops, looks down at me, and there's a softening in his eyes. "Please, Jasmine. In a moment, you'll understand."

It's hard to refrain from stomping my foot. "What if I want to remain ignorant?"

"Do you?" His eyes rise in challenge. "Not like you, Jasmine, to turn away from having all the information."

I might not have ever expected this career path, but I've become an author. I spend my life weaving plots, trying to understand motivation and emotions. Suddenly, I realise that no matter how uncomfortable I am, if I walk away now, I'll always wonder why Strider thought it so important I meet his wife. Though right now, I can't fathom any reason for it.

Unless... Has he an open marriage and his wife won't mind? Or, *God help me, no.* I narrow my eyes. "I'm not into threesomes."

His eyes widen so far, it's comical. His mouth drops open, then he recovers himself. There's even a quirk to his mouth. "Just get inside, Jas." After a pause he adds, "Please."

Something about his tone, or maybe his countenance, stops my protest. For some goddamn reason, deep inside, I still love the man even though I know he doesn't—and shouldn't due to his marital status—feel the same for me. Even though thinking I'm an idiot to put myself through this torture, I find myself beside him as he puts the key in the lock, turns it, and opens the door.

"That you, Colt?" a feminine voice calls out. She uses what I assume, but hadn't known, was his government name, which emphasises the vast gap between her and me.

He barks a laugh. "Who else would it fucking be?"

That's his wife, I remind myself and start panicking. *How bad will this be?*

The door closes behind me with a decisive click. I've no option now but to follow his lead. With his hand on my back, he encourages me forward into the room where the voice came from.

I come to an abrupt halt at the sight in front of me.

There's a woman in a wheelchair, held in by straps, as if her body is incapable of supporting itself. Apart from her chest gently rising and falling, there's no other movement, no recognition that anyone has entered the room. Beside her stands another woman clothed in a nurse's uniform. It's her that's giving Strider a welcoming smile.

"How is she today?" the man beside me asks.

"As comfortable as I can make her," the nurse replies. "Are you going to visit with her awhile?"

Strider gives an abrupt nod. The nurse gets up. "I'll be in the kitchen if you need me."

I'm still trying to get my head around the dynamics in the room. Casting a quizzical glance toward Strider, he takes no time to enlighten me.

"Let me introduce you." He points to the comatose-looking woman in the wheelchair. "This is my wife. Anna."

I'm filled with horror. All my imaginations hadn't led me to this. I swallow, think whether I should temper my words, then blurt out anyway, "What's wrong with her?"

"Best diagnosis?" He looks at Anna studiously, then turns back to me. "Pick's Disease."

Taking a step toward the person he claimed as his wife, he places his hand on her forehead, smoothing the lines away gently. He stares at her for a moment, his face softening, then hardening as he turns back to me. "Come, let's sit." He beckons to a three-person sofa.

I perch myself at one end. He sits at the other but turns to face me. This situation is so far from what I imagined. For a moment, I focus on Anna. "Can she see or hear us?"

His gaze shifts from me. "Her eyes follow movement, but at this point it's unlikely she'd be able to understand what she's seeing. Same with hearing, she doesn't react to anything, even her name anymore."

Even so, I feel uncomfortable being here, especially seeing how Strider's expression gentles as he continues to stare at his wife. I'm just about to say I should go when he starts to confide, "Anna and I were childhood sweethearts. Right from the start, I knew she was the one."

His statement puts me completely in my place. There was never any room for me. However ill she is, he's letting me know I could never compete, and all my foolish dreams about him and I were doomed from the start.

If only he'd been honest with me. I couldn't have turned his approaches down. That was my bargain with the club. Sex for protection. But it would have meant I'd have shielded my heart. Knowing the truth would have meant I'd never have fallen for him. A cheater was never on my agenda.

Not understanding why he couldn't have simply just told me, I realise there's nothing more to say. Placing my hands on the sofa, I start to push to my feet.

He sees my movement and, stretching over, places his hand on my arm. "Please, Jasmine. I need to get this off my chest. Please spare me a moment. Just listen to me."

His tone is uncertain, almost vulnerable. If he had demanded, I'd have left, but his demeanour has me sitting back in my seat. When he doesn't immediately start talking again, it seems breaking the silence is up to me. "Will she recover?"

My question sparks him to glance sharply my way before he heaves a big sigh. Then he inches closer, taking my hand in his as though he needs a human connection. "No." I inhale sharply, but he's already moved on. "We were in high school together. When we left, I joined the Marines. Anna stood beside me all the way. She was so proud of what I'd accomplished, liked to show me off and boast about me going away and fighting for my country. And hey, what red-blooded man doesn't want his wife to look up to him? She worried about me when I was overseas, of course, but I suppose being the big brave man, I downplayed the risks that I faced daily. I did my time but couldn't do it anymore. After eight years, I got out." His teeth clench, and he moves his jaw side to side to release them. "I'd seen things no man should ever see and heard screams no one should ever hear. I could tell Anna was disappointed, but still, she stood by me.

"On US soil, I floundered. I couldn't find my place. Being a Marine was the only thing I'd ever known, and civilian life wasn't for me. Then I found the Wretched Soulz MC." He stops, considers me for a moment, then resumes, "Well, they found me. They threw me a lifeline, a way of living that I could understand, and once again, to be part of a team. Anna," he points at the woman in the wheelchair, "couldn't fathom what attracted me to the MC, and tried all she could to keep me away. Despite her objections, I knew this club was the only thing that was going to ground me. Fuck knows where I'd have ended up without my brothers."

Hie eyes glaze slightly as mentally he drifts back in time. "I'd come home a damaged man, unable to fit into society. Anna did her best, but she couldn't give me all I needed. I wanted purpose, direction. I tried to do what she wanted. At first, I turned down the Soulz approaches and attempted to live a citizen life. But something was calling to me, and I bought myself a motorcycle. Hell, how I loved the freedom it gave me. When Anna saw that, she knew that she'd lost.

"For a moment, she tried. She pretended to be enthusiastic about the bike, and when I asked her to come for a ride, she agreed even though I could see she didn't really want to. She rode stiff, scared, and, hell, I wasn't an experienced rider.

When a truck blew me off at a junction, I lost control and dropped the bike. She never rode with me after that, and since her, I've never had another woman riding behind me."

Something pushes me to ask. "Was she hurt?"

He grimaces. "It didn't appear so, but she had banged her head. Cops turned up, ambulance, too. They took her in and said she might have a concussion, but just told me to keep an eye on her during the night, and didn't seem to think it was serious. She woke up the next day with just a mild headache."

He laughs softly in a mirthless way. "She did use it to try to stifle my new desire for two wheels. For a while, I suppose it worked. I endeavoured to find a job, but how could you go from being a respected Marine to being a lowly mechanic with a man with a paunch who'd never seen action in his life spending his day shouting crap orders at you? Telling you how to do something you could do blindfolded." He shakes his head as mentally he goes back in time. "Anna saw it was slowly killing me, so, against her better judgement, when she got really worried about my mental health, when she could see there were no other options, she capitulated but made two stipulations. If I joined the Wretched Soulz, I didn't draw her into the club, and our marital life was to be kept completely out of it. The other?" Wincing slightly, he looks at me, then straightens his shoulders. "That we fulfil the original desire of us both. That we start a family."

Quietly I suck in air, pain lancing my heart as another nail is hammered into my coffin. He wanted her to be the mother of his kid, but not me.

Ignoring my reaction or not acknowledging it, he carries on talking. "I agreed to both conditions. I became a hangaround, then prospected, and got my full patch. True to my word, I kept her out of the club. Easy in some ways as I was never in danger of sharing club business with my old lady. She didn't want to know. She never wore my property patch, attended events, or came on rides. While I didn't set out to keep her a secret, many brothers who joined the club after me didn't know of her existence."

I can't help myself. I snort. "I bet that was hard. No one questioned you going with the whores?"

His move is just short of violent as he uses his grip on my hand to pull me around to face him. "I never cheated on Anna. I didn't take advantage of the women in the club. Anna was enough for me." He grimaces and looks away. From the sideways view, I can see his Adam's apple bobbing in his neck as he swallows. "Well, at that time, anyway." He coughs to clear his throat. "We were too busy trying to get pregnant. I wasn't wanting for sex." He huffs a sad laugh.

"You have a child? Children?" Christ, this is getting worse. Though I've glanced around, the walls are empty of any family photos. Just a portrait of him and Anna in much younger and clearly happier days.

A rapid shake of his head. "We tried and tried, but she didn't fall pregnant. She started to get depressed. I just thought it was because she yearned to have a baby. We went to doctors, but they had no answers. Give it time, they said, but still, whatever we did, didn't take."

And I fell at a drop of a hat... Guilt floods through me. I can now understand his reaction. Can see it through his eyes. He wasn't able to give the woman he loved a child, yet found himself getting a club whore pregnant instead.

I swallow my gasp as he continues without realising the effect his words had on me. "I wanted a child with her. Wanted to fulfil her needs. Then Rooster died..." His voice trails off, and he looks at me expectantly.

I take a moment to process what he said, then answer the unspoken question. "The old Prez?" I wasn't there at the time, but have heard his name mentioned and seen the pictures on the walls.

"Yeah," he confirms. "He was like a father to me. He *saw* me. He was the one who found a disillusioned retired Marine drowning his sorrows in a bar. He saw me as a damaged man, understood what I'd been through, and how much I needed the life and brothers around me. He waited until I'd come around, then sponsored me into the club. When we lost him, I couldn't believe it. It was so unexpected, I wasn't prepared. It hit me, all of us, hard."

Now it's me squeezing my fingers to his. I feel forced to say, "I'm so sorry." And I genuinely am. I cast my mind back to the stories I've heard, and what I'm looking for comes into my mind. "He had a bad bike accident, didn't he?"

CHAPTER FIVE
STRIDER

Assailed by memories, it takes me a moment to respond to Jasmine's question with anything other than a simple nod. Rooster had indeed lost his life, and devastatingly, not with dignity against a human enemy but a six-wheeler truck. A blown tire, rubber flying down the road, he had no chance when the debris had crashed into his bike.

A useless waste of life.

The shock caused despair throughout the club. Rooster had been a good man, one of the best, a firm but fair and well-respected prez. His demise, the type of which all motorcyclists face, nevertheless seemed too mundane for a man who'd always seemed larger than life.

I remember the silence when we'd heard the news. Brothers unable to come to terms with the loss, and then when the news sank in, they reacted in different ways. Some began to get drunk, relating ever increasingly overembellished stories of our late prez. Others put their heads together to discuss what the fuck would come next, the selection of a new leader, and a funeral to plan. Some fucked the whores, trying to celebrate being alive when it had been brought home to us how any of us could so easily die.

Me? I couldn't settle. I wanted to go home and make love to my wife.

I remember blaming the wind for making my eyes water on the ride. It wasn't the first time I'd lost comrades. I'd fought in a war and had witnessed men I was in action beside become injured or die, but Rooster's death knocked me for six.

Home, I'd parked my bike, almost forgetting to kick down the stand so anxious was I to get tactile comfort from Anna. My hand shook as I put the key to the lock.

"Anna?" I cry out as soon as I'm over the threshold.

"In here."

I'd followed her voice to the kitchen, my helmet and gloves discarded along the way. And there she stood, a vision for my eyes. For a moment, I couldn't speak, couldn't explain. Voicing the words and telling her Rooster was no longer with us seemed too final, too hard.

I no longer had to hide the tears leaking out of my eyes. My forehead was etched with lines of sorrow, and my utter despair was written all over my face.

Anna was fully focused on whatever dish she was preparing for dinner tonight. Her face scrunched as she concentrated on preparing some veg. She hadn't even glanced at me yet.

"Anna." I said her name to get her attention, my voice catching in my throat.

It had the desired effect. She looked straight at me, and I waited for her to ask about the devastation that was written in my features.

"I'm doing chicken. Is that okay?"

She hadn't noticed? "Anna, please." I walked toward her, taking the knife from her hand and placing it on the tabletop. I turned her toward me and pulled her tight, burying my face in her hair.

"I'm busy, Colt," she said.

"I need you," I told her, barely swallowing back a sob.

A squeeze of my hand reminds me I'm in the present, though my head's still lost in the past. It's like watching a movie as the scenes play out in my mind's eye. As if I'm the narrator, I start to speak.

"The club fell apart. It was so quick, so unexpected, so fuckin' damn senseless. I hung around for a while, but losing myself in a whore or drink wasn't my style. I... I needed my wife. Needed to reaffirm with her that I was alive."

Jasmine stays quiet, her fingers still tight around mine.

"Men don't cry, right? Huh, I was barely holding it together by the time I got home. I expected Anna to see how upset I was and to comfort me. Instead, she talked about the fuckin' meal she was cooking. She didn't notice my distress. And, even when I told her what had happened, she only frowned. There was no compassion, no understanding, and seemingly no comprehension of what I'd lost." I pause and take a deep breath. "I returned to the compound, lost myself in a bottle, and then, for the first time ever, I cheated on Anna and used a whore. I didn't return home for three days." I shake my head, wondering if I'd successfully conveyed how much I'd needed human comfort to cope with the loss of a man who'd proved so important in my life, and why the coldness of the one person left who should have been there for me was so upsetting. I risk a look at Jasmine but can't read the expression on her face.

I continue my story. "When I did go back home, I started to notice little things I hadn't really seen before. Anna and I were always demonstrably affectionate, but now she seemed to avoid touching me. We used to be able to have good conversations, but I started to think she wasn't even listening to me anymore. I began to wonder who this woman I was living with was. I even suspected news of me being unfaithful had reached her, but as she had no connection with the club, there was no way she could have known."

Breaking off, I huff, remembering my disillusionment at the time. "She was cold and distant. Home wasn't a good place to be. It started to feel like I was living with a stranger. I felt lost and began spending more time at the club. Then, for some unknown fuckin' reason, the brothers thought I'd be a good replacement for Rooster, so they made me the prez." I shake my head, a small turn up to my lips as I remember something actually good from those days. "Which meant I had more commitments and excuses for me being away from home. Truth is, I don't know if Anna even noticed." Pausing, I recall how Anna hadn't seemed either pleased or upset to learn of my new status and how, for a moment, I'd wondered if she'd found somebody else and had been playing away. "We'd drifted apart," I tell Jasmine. "Or at least, that's how it seemed to be. When I did go home, the place started to look neglected, as if she'd lost the will to keep it clean and tidy. Anna didn't work. We'd agreed she'd be a stay-at-home mom, but of course, that hadn't worked out. I didn't mind. I was happy to support her though there were expectations that she would play her part. I wasn't best pleased to find her wasting her days away without lifting a finger. She even stopped taking good care of herself. My pretty, proud of her appearance wife was turning into someone else."

Jasmine stays quiet, her non-judgement helping me to continue.

"Then she started fucking with me. She asked me to hand her an apple, so I did. She told me not to be so stupid and asked me once more. When I couldn't understand and just stated I was complying with her request, she blasted me, reached around me, and picked up an onion instead. I threw my hands up and left once more."

This time, I lose myself in my head for a moment, thinking back to all the signs I'd missed. All the blame I'd put on her.

I decide to cut to the quick. "I went back to the club. The only explanation I could see was that Anna wanted out of the marriage and was chasing me away. I lost myself in club pussy and drink. Until, one day, I needed stuff from the house. I went back to find the place in disarray, no food in the cupboards and Anna looking a total mess." I brush my hand over my forehead. "It hit me then she wasn't well. And fuck, the guilt I felt was like a kick to the gut. But when I said I thought she needed to see a doctor, she brushed me off." My voice trails off for a moment, remembering that conversation. "I pulled rank. Told her I'd leave her for good unless she saw someone. Made an appointment and took her in. The doctor listened more to her, who was saying there was nothing wrong." My hands clench as I recall how angry I'd felt then. "I got her to see someone else, and this time, they asked deeper questions and listened to me. They diagnosed depression and prescribed something to help. Only, it didn't."

"Was that when you got the diagnosis?" Jasmine's gentle voice asks. "What was it you called it?"

"Picks Disease." I let my gaze rest on my wife for a moment, and seeing the confusion in her eyes, add, "A form of frontal lobe dementia. But no, it wasn't that simple. It took two years for anyone to give it a label, and even then, it was with a caveat that it couldn't be proved until postmortem. But she had all the signs. Lack of empathy and losing her emotions. Gradually, parts of her brain were dying, so she lost the ability to associate objects with words. When I'd thought she was fuckin' with me, it was the illness causing her dissociation, her brain slowly dying. And I was the asshole for thinking of offering her a divorce rather than support."

I risk a glance at her. Jasmine's face is drawn, and if I were asked to describe her expression, it would be devastated. I know in that moment that had I been honest with her, she'd never have graced my bed. And I got her pregnant. I made her deal with the *problem*. It's not just Anna I'm guilty about, but Jasmine herself.

I needed her to see, to understand, but why? I'm not even sure myself.

Jasmine's clearly trying to digest all that I told her. I give her the space but am unsurprised at what she asks next. It's a question I've asked myself and the doctors time after time.

"What causes Picks Disease?"

I give her the only answer I can come up with. "Sheer bad fuckin' luck." Then, after a beat, I clarify. "Maybe as simple as bad genetics, but a lot of the time, it can be caused by a TBI."

"Had she ever had a brain injury?"

She had when she'd come off my bike. But it had been so fucking mild, the doctors dismissed it could have been the cause of it. Didn't change what I suspected in my heart.

Anna and I were childhood sweethearts. We got married. She stayed by my side when I was in the Marines, patiently waiting until I got out. I was in fucking love with her, wasn't I?

Shit. That's a question I try to avoid asking myself. Had Anna not gotten ill, would we still have been together? If I hadn't had the niggling doubt it was my action, me all but forcing her onto my bike, that could have caused it, would I have stayed with her? I'd tried so hard to give her the baby she wanted so much. But wasn't there a part of me that was glad it had never come to fruition? No. I love my wife.

I do.

My phone rings. I pull it out of my pocket. Seeing it's Buzz, I know I need to answer.

"I've got to take this," I tell Jasmine apologetically.

Jasmine looks stunned with all my revelations and simply nods. "Okay."

I get up, walk to the door, and leave her.

What Buzz wants to check isn't complicated and just needs a simple no or yes. I pick the right answer, deliver it, and then stand with my phone in my hand. It hadn't been easy exposing my life with Anna to Jasmine. I feel like I've been through an emotional wringer.

CHAPTER SIX

JASMINE

Strider's phone ringing breaks the tension, and honestly, I'm not sorry to have a moment alone to process everything he's thrown at me. But I am disturbed to be left with his wife. What if she has some kind of episode? I'm completely out of my depth. While I usually think I'm an empathic person, it's eerie sitting here with someone who looks more like they belong in the next world than in this. Her breathing is loud, laboured, and I can see the rise and fall of her chest, but otherwise, there's no sign there's an actual person in there.

What could it have been like for her? Did she know she was slowly becoming a living corpse? Did she understand what she was losing? And, as for Strider, I shudder and suppress a sob at the thought of watching the woman he was, and clearly still is, so in love with, simply fading away. It must have been torture each and every day.

He cheated on her.

He did. But men, women, fuck, all of us have needs. It's obviously been a very long time since she was able to satisfy him, probably years from what he was saying. Bikers are definitely not saints, and with all the temptation around him, I can't criticise him for not being content with using his hand. I'd think worse if he took advantage and got his rocks off with a comatose woman.

He read my book. And isn't that embarrassing? Why didn't he pick up one of the first three instead? The ones where I hadn't subconsciously allowed my inner cravings to seep out through my words. In this one, I'd known my characters were me and him, but there didn't seem any harm in imagining a future that I most desired. It was all in my head though. I knew my dreams were just that. Strider had pulled away and now I know with good reason. It had been therapeutic to write down musings, hopes that could never come true. Letting my fictional character enjoy what might have been. For just a short while, I'd allowed myself to dream.

Anna makes a soft sound that makes me jump, but she doesn't appear to have moved or show she needs or wants anything. *She's the reason Strider rightly couldn't commit to a relationship with me.* At least it wasn't something in me that was lacking, but a prior commitment on his part. I try to take comfort in that thought.

But where does that leave me now?

It's been more than a couple of minutes since Strider left the room, but that's nothing new. I know the business of an MC prez can be complicated and take up a lot of his time. It's one of the things I use to add detail to my books—the man at the top needs to be dedicated to protecting the club, which often involves sacrificing his private life. He runs businesses, both legal and those that probably cross the line, and is the backstop for all the problems his brothers might have. We've often been interrupted by a phone call or knock on the door.

I sit, my body tense, feeling uncomfortable, as my eyes flick toward Anna as though constantly checking she's still alive. I wouldn't be human if I wasn't consumed with compassion for her and such a waste of a life. I can't tell how old she is, but if she was at school with Strider, then she's the same age, making her ten years my senior, barely middle-aged.

"Colt's a good man." Startled, having been lost in my thoughts, I glance up. The nurse has returned and she's carrying a tray. On it is perched a cup with the aroma of coffee and some creamer and sugar. She places it in front of me and gives me a wane smile.

"I half think I should be offering you something stronger," she starts, then at my raised brow adds, "I take it you didn't know about her? Or at least her condition."

Eyeing the bounty put in front of me, I realise that she's probably right. I'm in need of some stimulant, but coffee will have to do for now. As I doctor the brew to my satisfaction, I answer her. "I didn't even know he was married." It must have been the way I all but spat out the words that caused her to give an exaggerated eye roll. It's clear she thinks I'm his bit on the side, so I hastily explain, "It has always been casual between us. Strider never made any promises or led me on."

She studies me, and I wonder what's going through her mind. Does she think I'm a whore, just a bed warmer? Well, then she'd be right. But rather than offering criticism, she checks on her charge, then returns to me, taking a seat on the armchair opposite. Rather than sitting back, she leans her elbows on her knees, places her chin on her hands and continues to make her visual assessment.

The silence starts making me feel awkward until, at last, her mouth opens to let words come out. "You're part of Colt's club?"

How do I answer? I give a shrug. "Kind of. I live and… work there." I hope she won't notice my slight hesitation, but if she probes, I can rightly say I'm a bartender for the most part. Considering the last few months, that's not a lie.

She seems content with that answer. "Hardly anyone from there comes around. And no one recently." Lines appear on her forehead as she frowns. "I see it as a positive step that you're here now. Colt's been dealing with this all on his own for a very long time."

Bowing my head, I shake it from side to side. "I think it's the opposite." Feeling no animosity from this unknown woman, I decide to come clean. "There's nothing between me and Strider, *Colt*. Or there shouldn't be. Both of us knew the score. Though he didn't tell me about Anna, he made it clear that we weren't in a relationship that was going anywhere." I swallow. There's something about this woman, maybe the empathy, that makes her a good nurse, but I suddenly have an urge to confide. "I, er, couldn't hide my feelings that I wanted more." Well, writing them in that damn book had made it obvious. "That's why he brought me to meet Anna, so I could understand we'd never be anything more."

She seems to ignore me, instead imparting more information. "Anna wouldn't be alive now if he'd done what most do and consigned her to the hospital. She'd have given up long before now." She stares at me, checking that I'm taking her words in. "He pays for full-time care. I'm just one of three nurses on rotation."

When she pauses, I think she's waiting for some platitude. I give it to her. "He loves her a lot."

The nurse gives a slow, non-committal nod. "He loved her once. But now? If you ask me, it's guilt that makes him give her everything he's got."

"Wouldn't anyone?"

"Hell no." She barks a laugh. "When it gets this hard, when the person loses all of themselves, hospice care is usually the option." She gives me a piercing gaze. "He hasn't brought anyone here before." She gestures toward the woman in the wheelchair. "Anna's not got much time left. You think you're here to see he's committed to someone else? I think it's so you can see what he's facing. Colt will need someone when she's gone."

Is she suggesting I wait around for someone to die before making a move on the man? Before answering, I consider. Maybe I have been hanging around the club, probably outstaying my welcome, hoping that Strider would notice me and want me as the woman in his life. His reaction to the pregnancy should have been a huge red flag, but I buried my head in the sand and hung on, trying to read something different in his reaction to what it really was. But by bringing me here, I can see how much Strider loves his wife. Being with me was only ever a way to satisfy his male urges, which she could no longer fulfil. And, dead or alive, she's always going to be number one in his life. While I'm unable to compete with a living woman, it's unlikely I'd ever win out over a ghost.

Coming here has shown me there's absolutely no hope.

I feel for Strider. My heart breaks knowing he's soon going to lose the love of his life. That he's not approached me for sex in months, that he's been avoiding me, shows I've become a distraction rather than a comfort. That's not going to change. Strider's got his brothers to be there for him, and Haley or Kat, the other club girls, if he needs his itch scratched.

I finish my coffee, pick up my bag and rise. "Can you tell Strider that I understand?"

She too gets to her feet and brushes her hand over her tidy hair. She sounds anxious. "Don't go. I didn't mean to chase you out."

"You didn't," I rush to reassure her. "I heard what you said, but I've received his message loud and clear." In my head, my plans are already made. I'll call an Uber, go back to the club, pack, and then leave town. A motel room will suffice until I find something permanent. I've got money in my bank account, and as long as I keep publishing books readers want, enough to live on, hopefully, coming in month to month.

Her hands wring together. "At least wait until Colt comes back inside and tell him yourself."

I shrug, and huff. "He's brought me here to explain why he can't offer me anything."

Taking a step toward me, she places her hand on my arm. "Don't give up on him, please. However much he wills Anna to recover, that's one thing she won't be doing. He'll need someone..." Her voice trails off, and I fill in the blanks.

But I can't be someone who can make up for the true love he's lost. I need to be wanted for me, not as a substitute for someone else.

Giving her a nod to show I acknowledge her words, even if I don't accept them, I edge out of the door. Casting my eyes to my left, I see Strider standing outside the back door. Turning in the other direction, I head out of the main entrance. I exit quietly, walk past the SUV, down to the fence, then walk another few yards before pulling out my phone to summon a rideshare.

How he can move so quietly, I'll never know, but a deep voice sounds from beside me.

"Running out without saying goodbye?"

Mentally, I'm already one step removed from him, the decision made to leave the club, and therefore his influence, though he'll never lose the respect I hold for him. Therefore, I don't feel like a child caught red-handed and make no excuses. "There's nothing more to be said between us."

Placing his hand on my shoulder, he swings me around to face him. "I brought you here so you could understand—"

"I understand, alright," I interrupt, not allowing him to finish. My palm finds his chest, feeling the fast beating of his heart. "I came to the club when I was desperate. I was prepared to do whatever it took to get sanctuary. But somehow, I was lucky enough to catch your eye." When he goes to speak, I shake my head. "It's not your fault. You made it plain all along, but I allowed hope to build up in my mind."

Strider rolls his head back and emits a long sigh. "It's not all on your side." He lowers his eyes, catching mine. "Anna's dying."

"Strider," I say as gently as I can. "I couldn't compete with the real woman, and I won't be able to compete when she's not alive. She holds your heart. I can't take second place, not now, not in the future."

At that point, the Uber I called turns up. It's my cue to leave, not to extend this, not to draw out the painful end to something that never really began. I hold out my hand. Bemused, he stares at it for a moment before moving to take it.

I give a quick shake, but he squeezes and holds on tight.

"No, Strider," I force myself to say firmly. "I hope you can find peace in your future, but I've nothing to offer you." Under my breath, I add the word now. Who knows what the years ahead will bring? Maybe at some point, our two lost souls might rediscover each other. But he's got his life to lead, which unfortunately includes watching his one love die.

He opens his mouth, but I reclaim my hand, step to the Uber, open the door, and sit inside.

I don't look back. With the tears in my eyes, I wouldn't see much even if I had. I don't know if he waited until I was out of sight or immediately went back inside.

As we approach the compound, I use a tissue to dry my eyes, apply some makeup to hopefully hide some of the redness, but there's no way to disguise the fact that I've been crying. Trying to keep my head down, I wave my hand in acknowledgment to a greeting someone calls out, exit the back of the clubhouse, and make my way to the room that I've lived in for the last three years.

For a moment, I stand at the door, considering the space. It's furnished like so many others—bed, closet, drawers, desk and a television on the wall. I made it my own with a colourful rug on the floor, and the cheerful bed coverings. It might not be much, but it's felt more like home than any place I've resided. *Because of Strider. And my foolish hopes.*

Telling myself I'm not the same broken girl as I'd been when I'd arrived, I draw out the shabby suitcase from under the bed and start to fill it with my clothes and personal items. It doesn't take long to pack. The last thing, my precious laptop, goes into my backpack. Glancing around one more time, I realise I'm leaving behind some of the stuff that made this room mine. *I'll leave it for some other club girl. Someone else to warm Strider's bed.*

Unable to continue thinking along those lines, I blink back more tears, then quickly go to the door, open it, step through and leave my key in the lock outside. I pause for a second. *Am I doing the right thing? Could I stay?* I don't see how. Strider will need space to manage his grief. It would be better if I wasn't around. Knowing what I do now, it would break my heart all over again if I was used as a prop to lean on. Straightening my shoulders, I grab the handle of my suitcase and swing around.

"Jesus!" My hand goes over my fast-beating heart. "Warn a girl next time, will ya?"

The massive form of Shotgun, leaning against the wall, as if he'd been waiting for me, vibrates with laughter. He grins unapologetically and nods toward my luggage. "Going somewhere?"

I sigh. "It's time," I reply.

He heaves in a breath, then sighs and hazards a guess. "You went off with Strider. He took you to see his wife."

Knowledge or conjecture? Well, either way, it doesn't matter. He doesn't wait for my confirmation.

"You might not think it, but you've made yourself a place in this club. You don't need to work on your back to stay here. Surely you must know that by now?"

My eyes widen as my head moves side to side. "I've been taking advantage. I've got my own career and can move out and support myself."

He shrugs. "Just because you can stand on your own two feet doesn't mean you have to. Hey, Jas, we all like you being here. You run things for us." His lips turn up into a smile. "I don't think you realise how much we've come to depend on you to keep the club girls in line, food on the table, and the right drinks on the bar. Why don't you stay, Jassy?" The last is said in a cajoling tone.

I'm surprised the offer is being made. All I've ever done is make myself useful to continue to have a roof over my head. I hadn't realised they'd appreciated me in that way. How much would it take to persuade me to stay? But as I feel myself weakening, the thought of Strider comes into my mind. How could I cope with seeing him around the club, knowing what a fool I've been.

I came here for protection. That was three long years ago. In the intervening time, there's been no sign of Barclay. It must be safe for me to leave now. Why would he still be looking for me? Yes, it's time for me to go. Time to build a new life.

As the thoughts go through my head, I notice Shotgun has taken out his phone and is texting, seemingly oblivious to my presence.

Great. Yeah, like I'm so important when he's clearly got other things on his mind.

Now, I have no reluctance in saying, "I need to go. It's time. *Past* time." I pull back my shoulders and take hold of the handle of my suitcase again.

He spares me a glance, examines the commitment on my face, then nods. Without words, he takes my luggage from my hand and precedes me through the corridor and out into the clubroom.

I come to an abrupt halt. There, in front of me, is Buzz, Tequila, and half a dozen other members. Their arms are folded, and they are forming a barrier between me and the door.

CHAPTER SEVEN
STRIDER

When I return to the club, it seems ominously quiet, as if you could cut the atmosphere with a knife. As Prez, I'm not used to being given the cold shoulder as I enter, nor treated to some of the looks of derision that are being sent my way.

What the fuck?

I'm really not in the mood for this. It's hard enough returning, knowing I'll see Jasmine while accepting I've lost all right to touch her.

I don't understand what I thought I'd get from introducing her to my wife. I just knew it had to be done. Jasmine deserved to know the complications I had, and seeing Anna would explain more than any inadequate words that could come out of my mouth.

In a different world, a different time, Jasmine would be mine.

I suppose I thought she'd wait, that she'd comprehend that I still wanted her around. But while I hadn't blatantly lied to her, I had let her think I was single and free to explore a relationship. She could rightly berate me for leading her on.

Straightening my back, I broaden my shoulders, ready to accept whatever the brothers want to bring. The expressions on their faces make me suspect Jasmine has got in with her side of the story first. I hadn't taken her for a blabbermouth. I hadn't explicitly asked her to refrain from telling all the brothers about my wife—of course, they know I've got another life. But that's far from unusual. Many bikers also lead civilian lives. Only my top team, the brothers who I've ridden with longest, know the details of Anna's illness. I'm not ashamed of it, but I haven't wanted any concessions made because of what I've got to deal with outside of the club.

I've prided myself on being an MC prez and a husband to a terminally sick wife.

Damn it. I never wanted my two lives to collide, but Jasmine might have spread my secrets far and wide. Though, as I glance around at the assembled brothers, no one's looking at me with the compassion I'd expect if they'd been told about the seriousness of Anna's plight. If anything, they look disgusted with me, making me feel angry inside. *How dare they judge me for making the best of the hand I was dealt, one I never asked for?*

Heading to the bar, I rap on the top when the prospect doesn't turn to me immediately.

"Jack," I demand once I have his attention. Then, casting my eye around, I don't see the person I'd prepared myself to see. "Where's Jas?" I snap.

It's not the prospect, but Buzz who answers me, his sudden bark from behind making me swing around as he repeats, "Where's Jasmine?" His eyes are open wide, and his head is shaking. His forehead furrows. "You know where she is."

"If I fuckin' knew, I wouldn't be asking."

"Well, she's not fuckin' here. She's gone." Clearly seeing my look of disbelief, Buzz's frown deepens. "What the fuck did you say or do to her, Prez?"

At least he's still giving me the respect of my title. I suppose that's something. Draining the shot of Jack in one swallow, I brush my hand over my mouth, glance around to make sure no one else is within hearing, and lean in close before I say softly, "I read that book you gave me. Knew she was developing feelings for me. So I took her to see Anna, show her why she had to shut those emotions down. That there was no way I could reciprocate them." Buzz has been one of my closest friends since I joined the club, and there's nothing he doesn't know about me. He's known Anna, met her, and knew she was always there in the background. Had been my sounding block when I needed to vent, first about my wishes she'd be more involved in the club, then was there for me every step of the way since her diagnosis a long ten years back.

His reaction isn't what I expect. "You fuckin' what?" Buzz shakes his head in disbelief, his eyes widening as he stares at me. "You're head over heels for Jasmine."

My mouth drops open. I thought I'd hid my feelings better than that. I never concealed that I was attracted to her. Sure, my monopolising her services, even after I no longer used them, was a huge fucking sign. But love? I open my mouth to deny it and find that I can't. I shouldn't. My loyalty lies in a different direction. Leaving aside the question of how Buzz can so easily read me, I explain why I must obfuscate. "I've got Anna—"

He doesn't accept it and doesn't let me finish. "You've got a living corpse. A woman you were going to divorce years ago." He rubs at the sides of his temples. "A woman you only stayed with out of misplaced guilt." Rubbing salt in, he adds, "A woman you fell out of love with *before* she got ill."

"Did I?" I hiss, the old argument resurrecting in my head. "I met her, fell in love. Married her. Then she changed. Sure, I was going to leave her, but had she become someone else because the illness made her that way?"

"You'd already married in haste and had started repenting in leisure," he throws back at me. "Don't bullshit me. I was there."

But it's an unanswerable question. How much of it was the blossoming natural animosity between Anna and me, and how much was her own brain changing the woman I once loved? Had it been me who caused it? This isn't the first time I've had this argument with him.

I try to get him back on point. "Where's Jasmine gone?"

His eye roll is admirable. "Whatever you hoped to gain by taking her to see Anna, you must have fucked up. She took only one message from it—that she is no longer welcome in the club." As I open my mouth to explain I said nothing of the sort, he tempers his words. "Or maybe the facts came as too much of a shock, the extent to which you'd been hiding things from her." He holds out his hands in a defeated gesture. "We did our fuckin' best to get her to stay, but she packed her bags and left. Other than taking her prisoner, there was nothing else we could do." Seeing me go rigid and my look of shock, he softens slightly. "She left on good terms with us, and an understanding she could always come back."

For a moment, I'm speechless. I need to speak to her. I need to explain. The loss I feel hits me like a blow to the chest. I take out my phone to call her. She misunderstood. I'd just wanted to show her why she shouldn't develop feelings for me, as I wasn't in a position to offer her a happily ever after. Not while Anna continued to breathe, and I couldn't commit to how I'd feel once she was gone. The last thing I wanted was for her to leave the club. The phone connects, but the ringing sounds quite close to me.

With eyes narrowing, I watch Buzz take the device out of his pocket and show it to me. "Club phone. She left it in her room."

My gut clenches as a chill goes down my spine and I spit out. "Tell me she took one of the club vehicles."

The tightening of his jaw is the only answer I need. "God-fuckin'damnit!" I slam both palms down on the bar. It's only a second before I yell, "Data. Get over here!"

Buzz steps back as Data arrives. I don't even need to open my mouth before he's answering me, concern lines etched on his face. "She's off the grid. I don't even know what name she's using now. I've tried the name she gave us but come up with nothing, and Frobisher is also a miss." He nods a Buzz. "I think you're right and she's using a new identity."

Why wouldn't Jasmine just be using her real name? Oh, I don't doubt she's got the smarts to do it, but the question is why. The only reason that comes to me is she hates me so much she's doing everything she can so I can't find her. *No phone. No trackable vehicle. No fucking clue where to start.*

Clenching my fists I feel emotions sweep through me I didn't even know that I had. Clarity comes to me, far too late. Buzz was right. Anna and my marriage was already on the rocks before Picks Disease hit. The love for her had already been lost. But the guilt that I might have been responsible was a weight I've carried far too long. And couple that with the one thing she wanted I'd given to somebody else, the pregnancy, it had completely fucked with my brain. I'd lost everything when I made Jasmine terminate her, *our* baby. All because I thought I owed it to Anna, a woman who by then, couldn't even tell down from up, let alone be able to understand what was happening.

Tequila joins our party. He nods at Data, who raises his chin back, as though they're sharing a secret only known to them. But when Buzz tilts his head, I realise it's a confidence shared by the three of them.

"Spit it out," I demand.

Buzz shuffles, then asks, "You really have no idea, do you? Just how much of her book did you read?"

The question catches me by surprise. Sure, the plot was engaging, but I'm no reader. And I thought I'd read far enough. "I stopped at the part when the heroine fell for the Prez."

It's my enforcer who breathes out. "I think you ought to read the rest."

Before I can comment, Buzz states, "I've read them all. You already know why. Club girl writing about an MC might let something slip. All the previous books were fine. Good, readable, but light. This last one though? It's deep. Dark. Smacks of autobiographical to me."

Tequila shakes his head, but his words are affirmative, he doesn't deny Buzz's assumption. "I thought that too." His face tightens. "I hope to fuck we're wrong, but if we're not? Jasmine is in deep trouble."

My enforcer isn't a man to make a crisis out of nothing. He's careful, takes time to weigh up all the facts and, to date, hasn't led me wrong. A cold feeling settles in my gut as I realise I can't dismiss their concerns just because I hope that they're making something out of nothing.

"Okay," I breathe out. "Tell me what's so bad in this book that she wrote."

"Best read it yourself, Prez. Don't take our word for it. See what you think of it, and whether we could be right." Buzz's raised eyebrow is a challenge that I can't turn down.

Perhaps he's right. Maybe I know the girl better than them and will be able to tell them it's all imaginings conjured up out of her head. I've never met anyone so straightforward before, what you see with Jasmine is what you get. How could she have a secret past that's full of danger now? No, they're wrong. And seeing it written in her very own words will cement my opinion I'm right.

With a raise of my chin, I reach over the bar, grab a bottle of Jack, and go through the back of the clubhouse and out to my room.

Book lovers would probably hate me, but in my haste to get to Jasmine after discerning the depth of her affection to me, I'd thrown the book face down, and still open at the page which was the last one I'd read. Seeing it now, I've broken the spine. I'm sure that won't make the list of my worst crimes and serves me well now. I've no need to search for the place I left off.

Swigging whisky straight from the bottle, I settle down, propping a pillow behind my head.

Jasmine can't have led a secret life or be running from a past worse than perhaps a jealous ex. It's not possible, surely? Laughing internally at my officers' interpretation of the fiction that surely came straight out of her head, I start reading her words.

Despite that I don't normally read for fun, once more I find myself drawn into her story. It's no wonder she's found success. Her writing flows well and her descriptions draw me in. The interactions between the club members make me laugh. Until... I get to the part when the fictional heroine's background comes out.

Drawing my legs up, I sit up straight as it slowly dawns on me that Buzz and Tequila might be on to something. I've already accepted, and as proved by Jasmine's own reaction, the first half of the book, her longed-for relationship with the MC prez was based on real life. Now, the amount of description and detail certainly looks like it's been written with the knowledge of someone who has lived through severe trauma.

They can't be right, can they? Surely, I'd have seen something in Jasmine, a haunting in her eyes that screamed of abuse. But then, I hadn't really looked at her the first few times I took her to my bed, far more interested in her other assets to spend time reading the emotions on her face.

Jasmine can't have described herself. If she has, it's unbearable. After a few more minutes, I have to toss the book to one side as it's just too fucking hard to read anymore. Hoping with everything I am that if this has been her life, she's overdramatized what she went through to maximise the angst in her fictional world. Brushing my hands back through my long hair, I conjure up a vision of the beautiful face I'd eventually come to know so well, wishing I had her in front of me to ask, did you really suffer? Was this your life?

Not one to look a gift horse in the mouth, I never thought to question why someone like her had walked into my club, prepared to whore for my brothers. She'd so entranced me that as far as I was able to, I took her as mine. She'd never been a club girl in my eyes.

Because she hadn't been one. If even half of what she'd written is true, she came to us for the protection clubs like ours offer to property and to hide. No one would think of looking for her here. Not someone born into the wealthy family she had been.

If any of this is true, of course.

It can't be. I stare at the book as though it could give me answers, but apart from offering more pages to read, it's of no help.

My officers were concerned that Jasmine might really have been telling her story. I can't afford to doubt the rights of their insight. *I can't afford to be wrong.* She might think time is on her side. That after three years, she'll have been placed in the past. But I've known bastards like the one described, and they never give up. *If* even half of her story is true, she's in danger.

I push up off the bed, striding to the door and go back through to the clubroom. I waste no time raising my voice. "Church, now!"

"About fuckin' time," Shotgun murmurs as he walks past me, quickly followed by Buzz, Tequila, Mex, Data, Shout, Radar, Madman and Shark. Horn and Hustler aren't around, but they can be forgiven for missing an impromptu meeting.

I give them a moment to get to their places and settle down, then bang the gavel. With all eyes on me, I point to the man at my left. "Shotgun. Want to fill them in?"

Grimacing, my VP replies, "You want me to tell them what a dick you've been?"

Snorts of laughter quickly die as Buzz slashes his hand through the air and then takes the floor. "This may be something. May be nothing. But hear the facts, then you can decide whether it's a life-or-death situation and whether we take it on as a club." His eyes meet mine for a moment, and I nod.

Shotgun raps his hand on the table, and they all fall quiet.

The Arizona Charter has got StoryTeller who can weave a good tale. We might not have similar, but my VP doesn't miss that definition by a mile. Far better than I could have done, he enthrals us as he tells about an author who decides to use her background for her novel. With only a quick glance my way, he describes the relationship between the club girl and the MC prez, and then goes on to the darker parts of the story, the bits that make my stomach churn and the whisky I've drunk want to resurface.

I force back bile as he comes to the end.

There's silence around the table that's broken only when Madman cackles. He thumps his fist onto the wooden surface.

"Good one, VP. You really think Jasmine's different from any other patch-chasing girl? She got her eye on our prez." He waves my way. "I suspect Prez told her to get lost when he saw where things were headed. Girl left because her nose was put out of joint."

My hands clench. In some ways, Madman isn't wrong. I've nothing to offer to Jasmine, but I didn't really think that when I returned to the club, she'd have packed her bags and would be gone.

It's Mex who gets his word in next. "Must admit, I've not read all her books—

"Surprised you can read at all," Shout butts in, causing a raucous laughter.

Two raised middle fingers is his response before he continues, "But I did read the one we're talking about. She uses her words well. Can draw you into her world." He taps his head. "I believe her imagination is where this is all coming from. I thought it was far-fetched as I read it." He frowns as if he might be missing something. "What I don't get is why you think she's relating her own life now."

"Because she can?" Tequila suggests. "She's got her readers believing the stories she weaves. Maybe she feels more confident. She's not visited therapists that I know of, so perhaps it's cathartic to get her history out, and safe because it's dressed up as something made up."

"Which she'd have gotten away with," Buzz jumps in. "Except for the relationship between the heroine and Prez. If that follows real life, why shouldn't the rest?"

I feel I need to point out, "Except I didn't claim her."

I swear Buzz mouths *idiot* under his breath.

"So why the fuck are we here?" Madman states. "That's the proof that there's nothing to this. Prez don't feel anything other for her than a hole in which to place his dick."

Rage rushes through me at his description. There's so much more to my relationship with Jasmine than that. But I'd be betraying another woman if I admitted I had feelings for her. Even so, I can't leave it like this.

"Your prez, VP, enforcer. and sergeant-at-arms give credence to believing she's in danger. So, we're going to treat it that she is until we know for certain." I give my best presidential stare at Madman, keeping my gaze there until his drops, then turn my attention to Data. "You found anything?"

With a loud cough, Data clears his throat. "I found Jasmine Smart." Just as I breathe out, *thank fuck,* he continues, "She died as an infant of three months old, thirty years back."

"What?"

"How?"

The questions come so fast that it's hard to tell who's asking them.

"Fuckin' fake identity. Just like in the book," Tequila gets in.

As the implications hit, I find it hard to draw oxygen into my lungs. The girl in the book bought an expensive new ID, which is proof that Jasmine did the same. One more reason not to dismiss the predicament it's possible she's in. "And?" I snap, eager to hear the rest. "Where is she now?"

Data's creased eyes meet mine. "Sorry, Prez, she's off the grid. Can't find her anywhere." His head moves side to side slowly. "I don't know where to start. She may have bought another identity and is using that now."

"Why would she change her name again if it's served her well for three years?" Buzz's brow creases.

Tequila shrugs. "Maybe she wouldn't, but here she was guaranteed a place off the grid with no questions asked. She didn't have her name on any rental leases, and we paid her in cash."

Shout raises his hand, and I give him a nod. "She must have a bank account. She got payments for her books each month."

"But in what name?" Data ponders.

Something hits me. "Frobisher. That's her pen name. Maybe she was able to set up an account using that."

Data shakes his head adamantly. "Don't you think I didn't try that first? Been digging, and there's no account for a Jasmine Frobisher, just like there wasn't a Smart." His hands brush back through his hair, the gesture showing his frustration. "We don't know anything about her, where she came from—even the little she gave us when she arrived, I suspect was a concoction to hide her tracks."

"Frobisher," I repeat, making Data's eyes widen.

Exasperated, he spits out, "Prez, already told you I've looked into that." He stands from the table and goes to bang his fist on the wall.

"Data?" I snap, getting his attention. "Buzz had mentioned she said her pen name was the maiden name of her beloved grandmother. Why would she make something like that up?"

Buzz lets out a long breath. "Good catch, Prez. Well, now, surely that's somewhere to start."

Data crosses his arms. "What? You want me to search for an old lady who happened to be called Frobisher before she got wed and one who has a granddaughter—fuck, even Jasmine might not be her real first name." He snorts. "Do you want me to limit my search to the mainland USA, or do you want me to make it worldwide?"

Completely straight-faced, Shout remarks, "She has an American accent."

I almost wish I had a camera ready to record our computer guru's expression at that comment.

CHAPTER EIGHT
JASMINE

The one thing that's lifted me up over the past couple of weeks has been the memory of how reluctant the men of the Wretched Soulz were to see me leave. Their concern had warmed my heart. Although nothing they said would dissuade me, I had left with my head held high rather than feeling I was sneaking out with my tail between my legs.

It had never occurred to me how much the little I thought I did around the club had been appreciated. If it hadn't been for the message I'd clearly received from Strider and my unrequited love, I could have been persuaded to stay. As it is, I need the time and space to pull the pieces of my broken heart together, to accept once and for all that the Wretched Soulz and their prez don't hold the key to my future.

It's all my fault I fell for an unobtainable man. It was only his tenderness toward me and the monopolisation he showed that made me stupidly dream that he could be mine. I can't blame him for not telling me he had a wife. Bikers are a different breed, and normal men's morals don't apply. It was all on me for having expectations.

Now I'm the one having to deal with the disappointment and find a new place for myself.

It's not the first time I have had to press restart and rebuild my life, a sort of return to factory settings, starting off with a clean slate. At least, this time, I've my self-made writing career to support me. Last time I ran, I had money with me, plenty of cash left by my dad. I knew, though, I had to use that carefully. One advantage of being around upper-class criminals is that some of their knowledge rubs off. First off, I'd have to obtain a new identity if I didn't want anyone to find me. I was also going to have to be very careful about who I used to help me. The wrong person would lead to betrayal.

I lucked out, but the process didn't come cheap. In going to the best and one I'd heard was assured of discretion, I had to pass over most of my available funds. But I'd needed the ultimate money could buy. I didn't just want a new driver's licence and identity. I needed a background that would stand up to scrutiny.

Katrina Aster née James had successfully become Jasmine Smart.

But what I'd paid out had left me with very little funds, no home, no friends I could call on if I wanted to protect the new me. I certainly didn't want to live on the streets. That's when I came across the Wretched Soulz MC.

I remember entering the club for the first time, as if it were yesterday. I was scared, but realistic. I had little to offer other than my physical assets, but it would be far from the first time that I'd been used without my consent. I'd hoped what I'd heard about motorcycle clubs was the truth—that if you became their *property*, they'd extend their protection, and that's what I wanted most. What did it matter if I had a few more rough, sleazy men climb over me? This time, it would be my choice.

Despite my worst fears, the Wretched Soulz hadn't been a continuation of my nightmare. They ended up giving me more than my wildest dreams. I'd made friends and discovered a new place for myself. And even if I'd had to fulfil my original intention to allow my body to be used, most of the men in the club wouldn't have turned me off. Of course, it was down to Strider that meant duties involving sexual favours were light. It was my own stupid fault that the feelings I'd allowed to develop for him had brought my new world crashing down.

The end, the drastic change in my circumstances, had come so suddenly that I had no firm plans. I'd jumped into an Uber and run before realising exactly how much I'd left behind. I've no transportation of my own. A club vehicle had always been available should I have need of one—so for now, I have to rely on buses and cabs. My first stop didn't take me far, just to a cheap but clean hotel in town where I hoped I could begin to move forward.

I hadn't even a phone. It didn't seem right to take the one the club had supplied to me, though I had made sure I'd made a note of all the important contacts. That's one of the things I quickly rectified. In today's world, a phone is a necessity, but I decided to wait before thinking about to whom to give my new number.

What good would it do to give the Soulz the ability to contact or track me? I have to put that part of my life behind me if I'm going to heal.

I feel deep affection for all the members of the club but need time to pass to find some equilibrium before rekindling old friendships. What would that even look like? I was the club girl who only opened her legs for one man. And that's the one person I don't want to come after me. I don't think I'd be strong enough to turn him away if Strider turned up at my door.

Even now, I feel myself weakening. *He might not be free now, but he soon will be.* Slapping the heel of my hand to my head, I try to get into my thick skull that he never wanted me. I was a minor distraction from watching the woman he truly loves die.

I try to look at the positives. For the first time since I married Barclay, I can think about myself, and not just as a matter of survival. As long as those creative juices keep flowing, I have an exciting career. In many ways, having my heart broken will help me. All the angst I've suffered in my life are now put to good use as I allow it to spill onto the pages.

For the first few days, I hide low, letting my emotions bounce all over the place. The dominant one—sadness for the Soulz I left behind—but there's a kernel of excitement that's beginning to grow as I realise I can go anywhere, be anything.

Mentally ready to move forward, I start looking for a place to rent. After looking for a while, I realise most in Austin are too expensive, and I question myself, is a city where I really want to be? When an ad catches my eye for a cute two-bedroom one-storey in a small town about halfway between Dallas and here, I start to feel excitement. Googling, I find the town has got everything I'm likely to need—a small mom-and-pop diner, a coffee shop, and a place to get groceries. It will be quiet, and right now, that will suit me.

I purchase a cheap car, then drive to meet the real estate agent. The place is exactly as described and perfect. Within a few days, I've got the keys and have signed a six-month contract.

It may not be forever, but it's space to breathe.

Apart from using it to make arrangements for my immediate needs, I've not used my new phone. But once I've settled in, I call up a number.

"Jasmine?" is squealed and almost deafens me. "Oh, my goodness. Is that really you? Where are you? I tried to call your old number, but one of the guys answered and said you'd left. He started questioning me and asking me if I knew where you had gone. I was worried, Jassy. We've all been."

"Yeah, it's me," I confirm unnecessarily when I can get a word in, a smile on my face at the exuberance in Sheri's voice. It's nice to know someone is pleased to hear from me. "I'm sorry I worried you. I didn't have a choice. I had to leave."

"Are you alright? Did Strider hurt you?" Obviously, I can't see her face, but I can imagine her frowning.

"He didn't hurt me as such." I pause for a second. "Did you know he was married?" If she had, as a good friend, she would surely have told me. I know there's a code of honour among bikers, definitely bros before hos, but with us women, I'd have hoped it would have worked the other way too.

"What?" Her startled exclamation proves her ignorance, letting me exhale a sigh of relief. "No, I had no idea. I don't think Jake even knows. He never said anything to me." There's a brief silence before she next speaks. "Oh, hell, Jas. What an asshole. He led you on…"

"No," I interrupt quickly. "It was a lie by omission, and the circumstances aren't normal. But as soon as I knew, I had to leave. I was an idiot falling for him, Sheri."

There's no point lying to her. She's called me out on my feelings before. And, of course, she'd read the same book that Strider had. "Well, of course, you did." She uses the no-nonsense tone that most women can call on when giving supportive advice to a friend. "How are you doing? Are you alright?" Questions tumble out of her so fast she makes me laugh.

"I'm settled," I butt in as soon as she pauses to take a breath. "I'm writing. It seems that angst is good for getting the creative juices flowing." I don't tell her that I'm picturing Strider every time I sit with my laptop to write. Especially when I'm writing a more intimate scene. "And I'm getting in lots of preorders for Motorcycles, Mobsters and Mayhem." A worry hits me. "You're still going to come and be my PA, aren't you?"

"That's great on the preorders. I knew you'd do well! And, of course, I am. Try to keep me away." She's quiet for a second. "I'll have Jake in tow, though. I'll be eight months pregnant by then."

Chuckling, I reassure her, "That will be fine. I didn't think he'd let you come alone." Especially after what happened when she attended the signing as a reader last time. "I even checked for you. Sapphire, the person running it, has confirmed colours are allowed to be worn as long as no fights are started."

"I'll let him know. I'm so freaking excited, Jas." Her voice rises in pitch again. "I can't wait to be your assistant for the day. When do you want me to arrive? Do you need help getting your preorders together? Oh, and have you ordered any swag?"

Laughing at her enthusiasm, which, to be honest, isn't far off my own, I let her know her help would be appreciated and very much welcomed. Then I tell her I've had bookmarks done and a few patches made up for my fictional club that I'll be able to sell. She has me in stitches when she suggests other items I could have on my table—all penis related, of course. Her ideas make me laugh until my stomach hurts.

We finally end the call, promising to firm things up for meeting the day before the signing next month.

I do make her promise not to tell anyone other than Story-Teller that we've been in touch, and under no circumstances to give out my number.

From what she said, Strider's been looking for me. I may

think myself strong, but I don't know how I'd react if I saw him again. I think I'd weaken and allow myself to go back to being his prop.

Three years ago, I was happy to be used for just sex. But now I know I deserve so much more.

One day, perhaps, I'll find a man who wants me and not as a substitute for the real love in his life.

CHAPTER NINE
STRIDER

Anna might still be breathing, but it's only a matter of time. I've long passed the point of denial, of disbelief that there was no cure, no hope, and nothing but a death sentence. What I had with Anna is now in the past. I still hold great affection for her. Even with my current doubts, it could still be called love. It's been a very long time since it was the heart-racing, blood-pounding emotion that I once felt for her. She's no longer able to wear her wedding band, her fingers too shrivelled. It's been years since I wore mine, having taken it off when I thought divorce was what I wanted. Even when I knew that it was the illness that had taken the woman I married from me, I couldn't regain sufficient feeling to show any visible claim that I was hers. The symbol of our vows, which we'd meant every word of when said at the time, are now a mockery. *To death 'til we fucking part. In sickness and health.*

The death part? Well, I'd always thought that were more likely to be mine. That I'd be the one to go first. I ride a motor-cycle for a start, the risk compounded by being a high-ranking member of a notorious club. The sickness part? I was sure we had years, decades before we'd need to worry about that. We were young, and healthy. It would be a long time before we would be stricken by old age. And if something like cancer hit us, we'd be able to do everything to fight. Treatments were improving all the time.

But fucking Picks Disease. How could we tackle that? It hadn't just taken her life. In some ways, that would have been kinder. It had taken her from me, and from her? The ability to enjoy anything she once loved, including our marriage.

Before she'd become the complete shell of the person she is now, sometimes, in the night, her hand would reach for mine, squeezing my fingers. I allowed myself to believe in those moments that she was still in there, fighting to come out the other side. Maybe she had been, but even those small signs faded with time.

It's been so long since she showed any signs of recognising me.

There's no way back and only one way this can end. I'm just punishing myself for wanting to leave her.

It guts me now that Jasmine might have offered me a future, but my guilt chased her off. I fucked up and sent the wrong messages when I'd taken her home and introduced her to my wife. I suppose I'd gotten so used to Jasmine just being there that I didn't expect her to take such a drastic action. Probably, I, in a very male way, thought she would stay at the club because life held nothing else for her. Even if I'd known about it, I probably wouldn't have considered her writing to be anything other than a cute hobby. Of course, I'm proud as fuck to know she's got a way to support herself, but selfishly can't help but wish her books hadn't proved a success because then she wouldn't have been able to run.

Two weeks pass, and it's absolutely killing me not knowing

where she is and what's happening to her. I'd have been a wreck even without my fears about her past and whether it might catch up with her.

I have to force myself to stop ranting at Data as he's looking for the equivalent of a needle in a haystack and clearly doing his best, but it's hard to keep my temper when he's getting absolutely no results.

I'm working in my office trying to listen while Shotgun takes me through the finances of our businesses, finding it hard to work out from all the figures thrown at me whether they're healthy or not, as he's only got half of my attention.

Where is Jasmine, and is she safe? I'd felt like I'd been kicked in the stomach when I realised that unless we found her, I'd never know if she was dead or alive—unless her demise was newsworthy enough to be reported. And fuck knows, I'd hate it to be anything as bad as that. But that's the harsh reality of it. It appears Jasmine had successfully pulled off a disappearing trick once before, and if she doesn't want to be found, I may have seen the last of her.

With my hands clenched beneath the desk, while my head gives the occasional nod up and down to reassure Shotgun he's not wasting his time, I can't stop worrying about her. I realise as days go past, I probably haven't lost this chance with her, but any chance I ever had. I'd never be able to tell her the depth of my feelings nor have an opportunity to put things right.

Shotgun clears his throat. As if I've been paying close attention, I gesture at the tablet he's holding. "Carry on."

His eyes widen slightly, then his expression is shuttered. I think he knows I probably haven't digested one word he's said and that I'm just going through the motions.

My phone rings. Glancing down at the caller, I hold up my hand, stopping him mid-flow. "Gotta take this." His chin jerks toward the door, but there's not going to be anything secret about this. "I'll only be a moment." I've recognised my home number. One or the other of Anna's nurses, who's on duty at the time, has often called me, usually when we're running out of something she needs or if they think she needs to be seen by a doctor. The latter is unfortunately happening more and more, and my answer is always, *of fucking course.*

"Yeah?" I ask questioningly into the phone.

"Colt. I'm sorry, but Anna's got a very high temperature. I didn't want to wait, so I called the doctor out. She's on oxygen, but it's not helping much. She's developed pneumonia. The doctor wants to take her to the hospital, but I wanted to check with you about that."

Inwardly, I know we've come to the end. My breath shudders as I breathe in. However much you think you've prepared yourself, it seems you never have. "Can she be treated at home?"

I hear muffled voices at the other end of the line, and then a masculine voice I recognise comes on the phone. "Mr. Harman? It's Doctor Barker. I'm afraid your wife is very poorly."

"It's time?" I know the medic. He's been treating Anna for a while now. I've paid a fortune for him to make house calls instead of her being moved from the environment she's happy in.

He doesn't try to sugarcoat it for me. "I'm afraid she's not strong enough to recover. Let me take her in and make her comfortable."

Closing my eyes for a second and then giving a sigh, I offer an emphatic, "No." I pinch the bridge of my nose as I try to explain my answer. "What can you do in the hospital that I can't do at home?"

For a moment, the doctor doesn't answer. Medical staff, in my experience, like to be in charge of who lives or dies. But there's nothing he can say that will persuade me it's best to let Anna spend what little time she has left in some sterile hospital room without anything familiar around her, even though she may not be conscious of them at all.

When he does speak, he talks about monitoring, intravenous medication and tube feeding, all of which she's had at home for a while. But even he is half-hearted about the benefits hospitalisation can offer. I've had this discussion with him before. Without the enrichment of her home situation, Anna wouldn't have lasted as long as she has. The only thing he can do in a hospital better than the nurses at home is if her heart stops beating and she needs resuscitation. But as nothing exists of Anna now, to extend her life artificially would be cruel and of no benefit to anyone.

After her diagnosis, I'd spent weeks, months, even years hoping the doctors had gotten her prognosis wrong or that some miracle cure would suddenly emerge. Even though the medical profession is developing more understanding of the causes of types of frontal lobe dementia and has discovered the cause of Picks Disease is a faulty gene, any developing gene therapy would come too late to reverse Anna's condition.

And, if I suspected that the accident on the bike had implications more serious than anyone had thought at the time, this long after, there was no injury that could be repaired.

I've known this was coming for a very long time. So why does Anna's impending death hit me like a twenty-ton truck travelling toward me at sixty down the highway? Again, I think selfishly that I'd have liked to have Jasmine to lean on, but she's gone, and I have to face it's unlikely I'll see her again. Maybe it's the double whammy of losing both women in a short period of time, but I feel like something inside me has broken.

After only a little more discussion that I don't pay much

attention to, I end the call with the doctor, him not having convinced me and reluctantly agreeing Anna will stay where she is.

"Go home, Prez. Be with your wife." I'd almost forgotten Shotgun had borne witness to the conversation. As I open my mouth, he continues, "I'm your VP, Prez. I can handle things for a while."

I grimace, both hands pushing back my hair and holding it for a second before letting it flop back around my shoulders. "I don't know how long this will take." There can only be one outcome, but whether it be hours, days or weeks, it's impossible to tell.

"Whatever." He shrugs. "You need to be with Anna now. If we need you, we know how to get hold of you."

He's right. I've been on this journey every terrible step of the way with Anna, and I need to see it through. Though she won't know that I'm beside her, I couldn't live with my conscience not to be there with her.

Abruptly standing, I take my bike key out of my pocket, bouncing it in my hand. "Tell the others." It's a stupid instruction. Shotgun will do what needs to be done. "And..." I pause, wondering whether, under the circumstances, it's right to add my next words, then decide I don't give a damn one way or another. "If there's anything, any news about Jasmine," *good or bad,* I think in my head, "I want to be informed immediately."

There's no judgement in his eyes when he raises his chin.

As I ride out of the compound, leaving my brothers in my rearview, I'm unable to analyse my own frame of mind.

It's not unusual for a biker to live both a club and civilian life, and never the twain shall meet. When I first joined the club, they knew I had a wife but respected I wanted to keep my private life apart. Whether they knew or suspected she didn't approve of the biker life didn't matter. The bro code rules.

Whatever happened in the club stayed in the club, and if I was fucking around while married, no one gave a shit. It was only my closest brothers who knew about Anna's decline and devastating diagnosis. I wanted no pity given, no accomodations made.

My woman hadn't wanted to be a part of the club, hadn't wanted to ride up behind me, and never supported me as a biker. Her being ill made no difference to that.

It had meant no one noticed she hadn't been around. And, apart from Buzz, Shotgun and Tequila who'd always been my best friends and who'd stepped up as my trusted officers when I was elected prez, I suspect most thought Anna and I had separated long back.

I went home to my wife, leaving my brothers to explain my absence. I sat beside her as she struggled for breath. Her laboured inhalations belying a strength that was no longer hers. It didn't take long. Gradually, her body shut down, and it was only two days later that I saw her chest move for the last time.

It was a few hours before I moved from her side. In the silence, I'd reflected on our life. Nearly twenty years of marriage, the last ten spent watching her decline. How could I regret staying with her? If I hadn't been there, no one would have watched over her, seen to her comfort, and made sure she had every chance at some sort of life. I can't help but ask myself, would things have been different if we had had a child? Would having someone depending on her have stopped her going downhill so fast, or would there just now be a son or daughter who'd grown up living with but unable to know who their mother really was, who she'd been when we'd first fallen in love?

Eventually, I reached for my phone and updated Shotgun.

It was then it was brought home to me, if I'd needed confirmation, that bikers are a family. Shotgun and Tequila had quickly arrived, and over the next few days, it was them who'd arranged the funeral and for Anna's medical equipment to be removed from the house. Even though I wasn't sure whether I'd want to continue to live in this now-empty residence, they'd commandeered the prospects and club girls to transform the rooms, which had more resembled a hospital ward for the last few years, into a comfortable home.

Although to many of my brothers it came as a surprise that I'd still been with my wife, once apprised of the situation, they ignored her feelings about the club and, for me, stepped up and treated her passing with all the respect that should be given to a president's old lady.

While her family had gone, and mine had long ago disowned me, her funeral service was packed, with a motorcycle entourage that encompassed not only the Texas charter but representation from Wretched Soulz far and wide. Even Slugger turned up, the shadow head of the entire MC. For once, he stayed in the background, waiting until her body was laid in the ground, and only then approaching to lay his hand on my shoulder and offer condolences, which I had no doubt were sincere.

I'd always regretted how Anna had never embraced my MC family, but never as much as I did now. In death, it had shown how much, if she'd allowed them to, they would have taken her to their hearts.

After Slugger took his leave, I'd stood by her grave, my brothers allowing me the solitary moment to consider the might have beens. But however much I wanted to summon up a rosy picture that if she hadn't been ill, she'd have eventually come around to my way of life and have been proud of me gaining the president's patch, I had to admit it was unlikely. Knowing Anna, nothing would have brought her around.

Now, she was gone.

Jasmine was still, hopefully breathing.

Not for the first time, I mentally kicked myself for the fool that I'd been.

Jasmine never asked me for anything. It was me who'd commandeered her loyalty, and she'd never questioned it. She'd given me everything I asked for. Even though, from her writing, it was clear she wanted more, she'd never pushed or demanded. I'd taken so much from her, including our baby. I'd made her sacrifice everything.

And what for? A misguided allegiance to a woman who, if she hadn't become ill, I couldn't see myself spending my life with.

I've been a fucking idiot.

The slight possibility that I'd caused Anna's illness had filled me with guilt. I could have just made it up to her by doing what I did, caring for her when she was ill. I didn't have to sacrifice my happiness for her, but that's what I did.

I can only hope Jasmine won't suffer because of my choices.

Out of respect for me, the brothers held a wake for Anna back at the clubhouse, but due to her distancing herself from the major part of my life, there were no fond anecdotes or stories to tell. It was a strange affair, really just another party night, were it not for the number of times my back was slapped and sympathies given as though I was dealing with a sudden hole in my life.

To be honest, my mourning had been done years ago, once I finally accepted her prognosis and the first time she'd looked at me with no real recognition in her eyes.

While they hadn't known her, my brothers gave me opportunities to regale them with tales about her, but I hadn't anything to share. My memories of her were too tied up in her medical issues, and all I could feel was a relief she was no longer suffering.

While it seems wrong to admit it, the weight of Anna had been lifted from me. After the funeral and the wake, my shoulders felt lighter than they had for years. Pastors would tell me Anna was in a better place. I might not be able to subscribe to that, but better must equate to the living hell she'd been in.

I no longer needed to worry about Anna, and that's something I hadn't been able to say for a very long time.

When I'd married Anna, we were young, starry-eyed, and thought everything was in front of us. Then I found my future, the club, and Anna rebelled. It was then I realised her dreams weren't mine. I could never become a nine-to-five office worker. I was a rebel, a biker at heart. I'd tried to make things work, tried to keep our lives separate, fuck knows there were enough examples around us, bikers with a civilian wife who they kept on the outside. Admittedly so they could enjoy the sweet butts and sex with no one turning an eye. That wasn't my reason. I didn't fool around on Anna, or not until she was unable to give me what I needed anymore.

Had I been an idiot to think if she wasn't ill, she'd still be mine? What would that look like? If someone had poured a bucket of cold water over me, I couldn't have been more shocked to find my thoughts had evolved. Anna and I could never have made it long term. If she hadn't become ill, there was no way in heaven or hell that we'd be together now. The club, to me, was everything.

Clarity suddenly hit. My guilt that I'd forsaken her due to the illness she couldn't control evaporated at the realisation I'd given her everything I could—a supportive husband and a comfortable life when hers went so rapidly downhill. I hadn't washed my hands of her, had tried to enrich her existence, had given her every comfort I could. Even if the cause of her illness had been my fault, it was over now, any debt to her repaid.

With that gone, I was consumed with thoughts about Jasmine. However much I tried to get her out of my mind, it killed me to think I'd pushed her away. I couldn't take comfort in the thought that if I couldn't find her, then no one else could. I was unable to listen to the sensible voice that tried to convince me the anonymity that stopped me from finding her would mean she was safe from anyone else. That book played on my mind. If what she'd written was true, she was in deep trouble, though she might not realise it.

I'd move heaven and earth to help her.

The brothers gave me space, but they couldn't tell it wasn't grief I was feeling but despondency and helplessness.

Avoiding the house, I took up residence in the club, feeling Jasmine's ghost everywhere. I wanted her so much. I thought I was going out of my mind. Someone can't just disappear, can they? Instead of accepting the inevitable that I wouldn't find Jasmine if she didn't want to be found, I sank deeper and deeper into despair.

It was two more days before Data burst into my office.

I sit up fast, reading the expression on his face. "You've got news?"

He sinks down into the chair opposite my desk. "We've all been fuckin' idiots. You included." At his accusation, I clench my fist.

"What the fuck are you talking about?"

His eyes roll. "We don't know where she is now, but we do know where she'll be in three weeks."

My brain's gone blank. I don't have a fucking clue what he's suggesting. "Spit it out, Brother." I'm losing patience.

Data grins, his cheeks pulling back, his lips curling,

showing his teeth. "At the book signing. Motorcycles, Mobsters and Mayhem."

My brow rises.

"I left my search of J Frobisher going and came up with gold. Jasmine's on the list of attending authors."

I've heard of that event before. "Isn't that the signing where StoryTeller's woman picked up a book that started their relationship? The one that saved her from a bullet?"

"Sure was." Data agrees. "It's a big signing. Must be a big deal for Jasmine to be invited to it."

Jasmine. My Jasmine. I knew she was talented from reading just that one book. For a moment, I allow myself to feel pride at how successful she is. But then, I consider the more important issue. This might be the break we were waiting for, but I refuse to get my hopes up. "How do you know she's still going?"

Data's grin widens impossibly. He thumps his hand down on my desk. "Because she's fucking asked StoryTeller's woman to go with her to help. And StoryTeller will be there because he's not going to let his eight-month pregnant ol' lady be anywhere without him."

My eyes widen. "You're telling me that…" I pause, casting my mind back, trying to remember the name of StoryTeller's girl. "Sheri, isn't it?" At Data's up and down movement of his head, I carry on, "That Sheri knows where she is?"

He holds up his hand. "Whoa there, Prez. I spoke with StoryTeller. His ol' lady doesn't have an address—"

In exasperation, I shake my head. "A number then. She must be in touch with her somehow."

"She has her number but doesn't want to betray a confidence."

My fist bangs down on the desk. "StoryTeller should get her under control and beat it out of her. I need that number.

It's fuckin' bro code, not hos." I punctuate my words by repeating the action of my hand hitting wood.

Data rolls his eyes. "Sometimes it's hard to believe you were married."

"Low fuckin' blow and too fuckin' soon," I snarl at him. But he does make me think. Yeah, in the early days, I picked battles carefully with my wife, soon learning like any husband, you didn't demand. You asked. Marriage was about give and take. But fuck it, StoryTeller should know where his loyalty lies.

Data lifts and lowers one shoulder. "Sorry, Prez." He doesn't sound particularly contrite. "Look, it's not an immediate matter of life or death. If I can't find her, it's a good bet that no one else can. If there is a risk, then it will be when she comes out of hiding to go to that book event."

It's not what I want to hear. I'm not a patient man. While I trust Data, I can't prevent the doubt curling inside me, souring my stomach that he might be wrong. What if that fucking husband of hers knows more than we think he does? What if we're sitting here twiddling our thumbs, waiting for her to turn up at the signing, but she never comes?

A large part of me wants to go to Arizona and shake the details out of StoryTeller's wife. She couldn't blame her husband if I was the one to do it, could she? On the other hand, that would get me a well-earned beatdown from her man, and maybe even Chaz, the prez of that club.

I finally settle for the one thing I can do. "Get back in touch with ST," I demand. "Tell him to make sure Sheri keeps in touch with Jasmine. The second she thinks something's not right, all bets are off."

Sensing the meeting is over, Data stands, a flick of his hand letting me know he's going to comply.

CHAPTER TEN

JASMINE

THREE WEEKS UNTIL MOTORCYCLES, MOBSTERS AND MAYHEM...

Pinching myself, and not for the first time, I confirm I am awake and not dreaming. It doesn't seem long since I envied Sheri for going to that amazing event as a reader, and now I'll be attending as a signing author. Can life get better than this? Oh, it could, I might have a man like Strider by my side, but for now, I'll concentrate on the good things and try not to miss what I can't have.

Three weeks. On one hand, the time's dragged. On the other, it's flown by far too fast. Looking down the list of the authors attending, I feel like an impostor. *How could my books ever be as good as theirs?* It's like the royalty of motorcycle club romance writers, and I'm not sure how I'll fit in.

My nerves are worse as it's the first signing I'm going to. I should have started with something smaller. I haven't a clue what's going to be expected of me, and I don't want to do anything wrong or make a fool of myself.

One good thing is that the online support from other authors has been magnanimous and so, so, helpful. It seems most can remember being a newbie themselves, and even some old hands are still courting advice about things I hadn't even considered. *What kind of swag do readers most enjoy?*

Eyeing the banner I erected in my lounge, I feel a sense of pride. It had only been from studying images of the last event that I realised it was needed. I'd had so much fun working with my cover designer to come up with something that had both my name and a slogan that represented my writing and with a, hopefully, tantalising background image.

Seeing *J Frobisher* written in such big words made me proud, but also made me question whether I'm suffering delusions of grandeur. Although I've four books published, I'm a baby in the author world.

When I go through the preorders, part of me is glad I haven't published many more. I can't believe the number of people who want the whole series to date. It makes me wonder how authors with forty-plus books cope.

My hands had actually shaken when I pressed the button, committing myself to purchase a large order for my paperback books. When the boxes had arrived, I'd nervously opened them, horror stories in my head of damaged copies or the right covers with the wrong contents inside. To my delight, and putting it down to beginners' luck, everything I'd ordered was present and correct.

Daily, it seemed, packages arrived with swag—pens, bookmarks, and the patches for my motorcycle club, with which I'm delighted. I've also got some bags carrying my logo that are big enough to hold each set of books.

I've thought of everything, haven't I?

A musical interlude interrupts my thoughts. Taking out my phone, I answer it.

"Sheri." I chuckle. "Your daily check-in?" I don't know why she calls so often, but I'm not going to complain. It's nice to have someone to bounce ideas off.

"Look, I'm living vicariously through you." She laughs back. "I'm beyond excited about going to Dallas. I can't wait. I want to be a part of *everything*."

"I'm not complaining. You've been so much help. Those pens you suggested will be great for signing the books."

"And don't forget the markers. You'll be signing shit all day. Readers had plush penises and everything last year."

She's my expert, and I doubt she'll be leading me wrong. She certainly hasn't so far. "Oh," I tell her. "Those penis lollipops arrived."

Sniggering, she asks, "Have you tried one?"

I snort. "I've managed to resist."

"You've got your banner, table runner, lights for the table and assorted swag?" She gets down to business, running through a checklist we'd composed.

"All ticked off," I confirm.

"Do you need me to do anything else?"

"I think we've got it covered for now. But, Sheri, please do keep checking in. It grounds me and helps. How are you doing?"

"I'm as big as a house. I can't see my feet now. I'm sure I wasn't this big with Maria."

I hear the sigh in her voice and work to keep the envy out of mine. *Foolish dreams.* "You know the sex yet?"

"No, we want it to be a surprise. But I'm leaning toward a boy as I'm carrying it differently from last time."

Briefly I wonder what it would have been like to have carried on with my pregnancy, but I shake that thought out of my mind. It's a rabbit hole I can't afford to go down.

Reference to her expectant state politely discussed, and

Motorcycles, Mobsters and Mayhem prep out of the way, we talk about everything and nothing for a few minutes, then end the call.

TWO WEEKS

ONE...

Going through what I hope will be my final preparations, I'm again interrupted by another phone call from the person who's given me so much help. "Yeah, Sheri, what is it? Have you thought of something I've forgotten?" I wedge the phone between my shoulder and ear as I skim through the piles of newly arrived books, sorting them into order.

"I think we've covered everything," she replies. "But I'm calling to ask a favour. Do you think you'd be able to fit another assistant at your table?"

It takes a second for me to get on board with the subject. "I've got a six-foot table, so it's possible, I suppose. I'll have to ask. Who have you got in mind?"

"Wweelll." She draws out the word then hesitates. "It's Helo. Chaz's woman." She huffs a laugh. "I didn't think she was the reading type, but she apparently has read your books and loves them. She's said she'd love to come along if there's space."

Helo is already a legend in the Wretched Soulz, albeit she's not an old lady in this charter. She was a Night Stalker, medically discharged, and now pilots a helicopter owned by the Arizona club. How she managed to tame Chaz, their president, I'll never understand, but apparently, she did. He's a beast of a man.

My mind suddenly starts racing. As a new author, I doubt

my table will be too busy during the event, and at down times, it would be nice to talk to the woman with such an intriguing background. Maybe I could star a Night Stalker in one of my books. I could certainly pick her brain. "I'll ask the organiser if she can come."

"Thank you. It seems to matter to her a lot." I hear the surprise in Sheri's tone but dismiss it. I find it understandable that anyone would want an invite to such a prestigious event.

After the call, I shoot a message to Sapphire. She's busy as all get out, so I'm grateful when, just a day later, I get a response and permission for Helo.

It's starting to feel all too real. As the day approaches, when I'll need to drive to the resort, I get more and more nervous. Sheri's daily calls kept me grounded, and I thank fate that our paths ever crossed. I don't know what I'd do without her doses of common sense. When I was looking for something suitable to wear, we FaceTimed, and I appreciated her invaluable advice.

Suddenly, the day comes when I need to pack up my car. Using my indispensable trolley—another of Sheri's suggestions—I easily manage to get all the boxes of books and swag into my car. I then pack my clothes, an outfit for the meet and greet, one for the signing, and one for the evening event. Wearing new jeans and a flattering off-the-shoulder top, I finally collect all my toiletries and makeup and manage to get my small case into my now crammed trunk.

Like me, Sheri is going to arrive a day early so she can check the preorders with me. I don't trust myself.

My stomach flutters with nerves and excitement as I drive to the resort. I'm excited to see Sheri again, intrigued to meet Helo, and above all, half terrified, half buzzing to meet the authors whose books I've devoured. I know I'm going to feel like a fraud among them. As for the readers? Hell, I'm going to be so nervous. People have actually preordered my books, and now I have to face them. Will I be tongue-tied? Will I make a fool of myself? Have I the right swag or sufficient to please them? Will they be disappointed when they meet me in person? What will they expect me to say? I'm actually glad Sheri's StoryTeller will be hanging around. He may be enough man candy to distract them.

My phone buzzes, and I put it on speaker.

"Hey, girl, it's me." Sheri's voice comes through loudly. "Where are you?"

Checking the GPS, I answer, "Almost there now. Five minutes to go."

"We'll be about half an hour behind you."

"Amazing," I tell her, genuinely happy that I won't be alone. "I'll wait in reception for you."

"Great. See you soon."

With no more to be said, we end the call. I drive up, park, then sensibly leaving my stock of books and other paraphernalia in the car until I can get Sheri's muscular man to help me, I wheel my small suitcase to the hotel entrance.

A wave of nervous excitement goes through me as I walk inside.

Like me, a number of others have obviously arrived early, and I recognise a few from their profile pics. Oh, wow. There's Amy Davies. She's come all the way from Wales in the UK. I have to fan myself. And is that...? Hell, it's only Winter Travers. Her books have been inspiring me for ages.

"J Frobisher?" An excited voice sounds beside me and hesitantly adds, "I'm Jessa Aarons. I love your books."

My mouth falls open as I openly fangirl. I accept the hug on automatic pilot while telling her, "You're one of my all-time faves."

A few authors I recognise as giants in the MC fiction world

I can't bring myself to approach and introduce myself, feeling too much in awe. But I'm pulled into conversations that soon have me able to suppress my nerves. *If all these wonderful people don't see anything wrong with a baby author like me being here, why should I doubt myself?*

Once at the front of the line, I get the key to my room, then turn around to see a very tall man pushing through the throng, clearing the way for a very pregnant woman.

"Jasmine!" she screams as she gets close.

I throw myself at her, remembering at the last moment to only give her a gentle hug. "It's so good to see you, Sheri."

StoryTeller coughs to clear his throat and then raises his eyebrows when he gets my attention.

Laughing, I put my arms around him, too, for a brief moment before pulling back. "It's good to see you too, ST. Especially as my trunk is full of boxes that I need muscle to help me with."

Sheri snorts and lightly puts her fist to her old man's arm. "She's got your measure, Jake." She chuckles.

Shaking his head, StoryTeller smirks, then flexes those muscles that are going to be useful. "Come on, then. Put me to work."

Indicating we need to fight our way back to the entrance, I follow StoryTeller as he again makes a clear path for Sheri so no one inadvertently bumps into her. I muse as I follow that most of the bikers I've met do not deserve the bad press that they get. They really are good guys at heart.

CHAPTER ELEVEN
STRIDER

’m mentally crossing off days on the calendar as if I were a child waiting for Christmas, counting down the time until I have a chance of seeing Jasmine again. I’m still working on a plan of how to engineer us coming face-to-face and practising what I can say when I get a chance.

I’ve missed her being around. Even the clubhouse seems less cheerful than it was. The bar is often unmanned, and minor fights have broken out between the club girls with no one to referee. It’s not only me feeling her absence. The atmosphere is different without her.

It’s not unusual to find copies of her books lying around, and brothers reading, or having them read to them. Or at least the salient parts. By now, even the most illiterate members know our suspicions about her past. It seems everyone has ideas, but none carry merit. Without more information, it’s hard for any of us to separate what might be real life from complete fiction. There’s a quota who think she’s exaggerating to make the plot more interesting, and others, like me, worrying she's watered things down.

I doubt Jasmine knows how much of an impression she made on my brothers. There's not one who isn't concerned about where she is and how she's getting on.

Now I'm heading into yet another church, knowing all eyes are upon me. If I hadn't fucked up, Jasmine would be here with us now. *Well, Brothers. No one can blame me more than I can myself.*

Data's hyped up. I can see that as soon as I enter. He can barely wait for me to get my ass on my seat, so I give him a nod.

"Mayhem's a fuckin' genius!" he announces, after my permission to speak. He then glances around.

My eyes widen in interest as Shotgun snorts. "Huh, the CIA, FBI plant in LA?"

Data seems incensed. "Whatever his background, he's loyal to the Soulz."

I raise my chin to support his assertion. The truth about where Mayhem came from or how he knows what he knows is buried deep under levels of security that only the man himself knows how to navigate. But Mayhem survived beatdown after beatdown as brothers doubted he was anything but a plant, and eventually earned the trust of those around him. I know his prez supports him, and if he's come up with something interesting, I want to know.

Cutting through the shit, I get down to business. "What has Mayhem found out?"

Data bounces in his seat, barely able to contain himself. "He's found who Jasmine really is."

"What the fuck?"

"How?"

"Who?"

Everyone starts talking at once. As the questions fly at Data, I bang the gavel and keep knocking wood against wood until everyone shuts up. "Let the man fuckin' speak," I growl.

Data nods appreciatively at me and starts to explain. "Mayhem's got searches that he can set up. They keep trawling on minimal data and then sift through the hits. All we knew was the name Frobisher, and that person was a grandmother." He pauses to shake his head. "How Mayhem found a needle when we didn't even know where the haystack was is a miracle, but we ought to be fuckin' thankful he did." Another break for breath. "Frobisher was the grandmother's maiden name to make it more difficult. But the long and short of the matter is that Jasmine seems to be a Katrina James, who got married to a Barclay Aster. Just like in the book, Katrina's father ate a bullet." He glances at me. "But unlike in her story, it looks like Katrina was in the vicinity at the time, which led to the police investigating her for murder. The case was dropped when only his fingerprints were found on the gun."

"She was in the vicinity?" I repeat, my eyes on Data. "You saying she fuckin' saw him do it?" What she'd written in the book was bad enough, but this? It's worse than I thought.

Data gives a shrug. "It's highly likely. Or at least, she was the one who found him."

Jesus. I wipe my hand over my face and concentrate on what Data is saying.

"Mayhem did some digging among his underground contacts. Seems Jasmine was married to Barclay to pay off Daddy's debts and he was holding Daddy's continuing existence over her head to keep her by his side. Then when Barclay didn't get what he wanted from her—apparently he thought she was barren and couldn't give him a child, he pimped her out to his friends." My jaw drops. It had to have been Barclay's fault. She'd fallen with me fast and despite precautions. But

Data hasn't finished. "Daddy somehow learned what was happening and it didn't settle well with him. Seems he thought taking his own life was the only way for her to get free."

Exhaling a breath, I lean back, swallowing down the bile rising in my throat. I always wondered why a girl like Jasmine would be willing to whore herself out to a one-percent motorcycle club. Now, it hits me that she was used to her body being used and was prepared for that to continue if it kept her out of her ex's clutches. "She came to us for protection."

"Would have been a fuck of a lot better if she'd come clean and admitted who she was and who she was running from," Shout growls.

Data's shaking his head. I raise an eyebrow toward him. "Reckon she thought we wouldn't have taken her in if we'd known. Barclay Aster is the fuckin' mob."

"And we're Soulz!" Buzz slams his hand on the table.

Mex taps his fingers. "Is there anything really to worry about? Daddy, who owed the debt, is gone. Katrina, or Jasmine as we know her, has been here for three years. Presumably, this Barclay has moved on."

Again, Data's head moves from side to side. "Barclay was legitimately married to her. Word is he wants an heir and can't get married until he can prove desertion, which has a few years to go yet. Also..." his voice trails off.

I grimace, interpreting the expression on his face. "And?" I don't think I want to know the answer.

After pressing his lips together, Data opens them to explain. "I don't think she realises it, but she was her daddy's sole heir. He might have had debts when he died, but he was asset-rich, and on his death, those could be realised. Barclay still wants the money he's owed. Mayhem says he's found evidence that Barclay hasn't stopped looking for her. And..."

again, he pauses, but I don't need to prompt him again. "Mayhem reckons he's probably got close to the same resources he has. Using the name Frobisher might be her downfall."

I draw in breath. If this Barclay knows what we do...

"He'll be waiting for her at Motorcycles, Mobsters and Mayhem?" Shotgun voices my thoughts aloud.

"Don't think we can discount it, VP."

I pick up the gavel, play with it, then slam it down. "Then we're going to Dallas. We'll be there in force. This Barclay will die before he gets his hands on Jasmine."

Buzz stands up, leaning over the table, pressing down on it with both hands. He stares me straight in the eye. "And why should we fuckin' bother?" he spits out. "Why pit the Soulz up against the mob?" He glances around the table. "Sure, we all like Jasmine, but she's just a club girl, and not even one who many of us enjoyed." His eyes come back to mine. "Tell us why we should put our lives on the line for this particular bitch?"

I get to my feet so fast my chair crashes onto the floor. Spittle flies out of my mouth as I tell him exactly how it is. "Because she's fuckin' mine!" I roar.

I'm not sure who starts the handclap, but in retrospect, I think it might have been Mex. But the sound of palms mashing together is repeated until it's a cacophony that hurts my ears.

"'Bout fuckin' time, Prez," Tequila shouts, banging his meaty palm down on the table and glaring until people lower their hands. "Now let's formulate a plan to get our First Lady back where she needs to be."

My old lady? Well, damn it, doesn't that sound right? Something settles inside me as I admit that at last. Okay, so maybe after everything, she'll take some persuading to throw in her lot with me, but I'll do all I fucking can to persuade her. She's no substitute for Anna. She's got her own place in my heart.

It dawns on me that I might be free, but she's not and won't be until… "We need to get Barclay Aster out of the way."

Shotgun raises and lowers his chin. "Doubt he's going to sign divorce papers. She's still married to him, and whether she knows it or not, she's an heiress."

"Is that an option?" Madman asks. "Look, Prez, you know we'll have your back, but the mob's not people to be trifled with. What if she agrees to give Barclay the money she owes? Maybe he'll back off."

Mex shakes his head. "Man like that won't want to lose face. If he's been chasing her tail for three years, he won't let her off lightly."

Madman's suggestion was a good one, but like Mex, I doubt it will work. I hate to admit it, but for him, it's cleaner if she dies, and then he'll gain from her inheritance. And with his connections, I suspect he knows ways he'll get away with it without her blood on his hands or her death being traced back to him.

Buzz clears his throat. "I think the question we should discuss is how we actually provide her cover." I raise my chin toward him. From experience, I know my sergeant-at-arms has something to say, and I want to hear it. "We can go en masse to the signing event, but it's not going to be easy for us to get close to her."

"It's not open to the public?" Shout asks.

Data shakes his head. "No, well, it is, but tickets were sold out way back. It's not something we can just turn up and enter."

"We might not be able to get inside, but StoryTeller will be going with Sheri, remember?" Buzz states, clearly getting to the point he was trying to make before Shout interrupted him. He slaps his hand down as though making a point. "We get StoryTeller on side and bring him up to date." He glances at

Data. "You got photos of Aster so he knows who to watch out for?"

As Data nods, I'm trying to process everything in my head. I don't like this at all. If my woman is in danger, it's me who should be there to protect her. But from what my information expert says, none of us will be able to attend the event except for StoryTeller. At least we'll have one man inside. While I don't like leaving anything to chance, it's likely her ex will come up against the same problem, and also be unable to gain entry. While Jasmine's in the resort at the event, she's probably safe.

But I don't like unknowns and not knowing the odds.

"I'm going to speak to Chaz," I decide and state. "We can then brief StoryTeller." I point to my right. "Buzz, get with Data and find out all you can about the resort when the signing is taking place. See where any weak points are. And Data?" I address the man himself. "Can you see whether Mayhem can check on Aster's whereabouts, and whether we can predict whether he's planning on visiting Texas?"

"Sure thing, Prez," both he and Buzz answer together.

"We'll meet back here tomorrow." I bang the gavel, then as the other brothers stand and leave, I beckon my officers should stay with me.

Once the room is empty, apart from Buzz, Shotgun, Tequila and myself, I go to collect my phone held in the box outside the door. Once I return, I pull up a number, click it onto speaker-phone, then put it on the table in front of me.

The ringing tone sounds a couple of times, then it's answered.

"Strider, Brother, how's it hanging?"

I sigh and get straight down to business. "Got a problem, Chaz."

"Anything I can do to help, you got it, Brother." He doesn't even let me explain before pledging to help. Not unexpected, I'd do the same in return. As would the presidents of the other Wretched Soulz charters.

It takes about ten minutes to fill him in, having to make time for his intelligent questions and a couple of inputs from Shotgun and Buzz. Tequila mainly stays quiet, listening. Then, Chaz takes a moment to think for himself.

When he speaks, he adds some clarity I hadn't considered. "Got a woman of my own now, as you know, Brother. So maybe I'm more up to speed on this keeping an ol' lady happy stuff." He chuckles softly. "Mind you, with Queenie, she'd have my balls if I upset her."

This is a very different Chaz from the one I'd spoken to a few months back. It's not so much that his old lady has tamed him, but perhaps made him appreciate some softness in his life. Though soft isn't a word you'd extend to Helo. My lips curve as I admit I'd think seriously before crossing her.

Chaz continues, "If I thought it would help, I'd instruct StoryTeller to get the contact details from his ol' lady and risk her wrath. But have you considered that if Jasmine's as savvy as you describe her, she'll probably have a burner phone that we might not be able to trace? And if it's a contract, who knows what name it would be purchased under. You said Data hadn't been able to find a bank account."

Well, I'll be fucked. He's right. Pulling my hair back, I hold it for a moment before letting it loose.

He hasn't finished. "She's still staying off the radar. If Mayhem can't find her, it's likely no one can. I think you've got the rights of it when you say she'll only be in danger when she appears in public at that Dallas event. StoryTeller will be there with her. I'll bring him up to speed so he knows what to look for."

"But will StoryTeller be enough?" I drop in. "I'm not

doubting his capabilities, but who knows what he'll be up against."

Chaz is quiet for a moment. "You said all the tickets are sold, and there's no legitimate way in?" I give an affirmative grunt, to which he chuckles softly. "You reckon Ms. J Frobisher would be able to have another assistant there? Or, if not, one who replaces Sheri?"

I breathe out. "I'll pick one of my men."

"Nah, I was thinking another female," he interjects fast.

"All I've got here are sweet butts—"

He bellows with laughter this time. "Who I'm thinking of will be as good, if not better, than any brother and definitely tops any club girl. If Queenie's willing to do it, then Jasmine will be covered for sure."

A startled laugh barks out of me. "You think Helo would help?"

"I think there's more question of how I'd stop her once she knows the facts. My Queenie does tend to get bored. Only one issue, she wouldn't be able to be there until the day of the signing as she's got a drop-off for me to do first. But that's when the public will be attending, so hopefully, StoryTeller can cover her himself until then."

"We'll be staying close by—"

"As will I and some of my brothers. Not leaving my Queenie exposed without backup."

All I can do is thank him profusely. We chat about arrangements for a while, then end the call.

There's a risk Barclay Aster will get to her before we do, but it's one I'll have to live with for now. Chaz had agreed that Sheri will check in daily and if there's a time when Jasmine doesn't answer her phone, she'll sound the alarm.

For now, I've done all I can.

CHAPTER TWELVE

JASMINE

I wake up feeling a bit fuzzy and regretting that last night I slightly overindulged at the meet-and-greet party. It had been an amazing time, getting to see and talk to other authors and some of the readers who are staying at the resort. While Sheri had backed out early due to her pregnancy, StoryTeller had stayed with me.

I'd gotten plenty of comments about the handsome biker who stayed glued to my side and, more than once, had to hastily correct the misassumption. I do think he was a bit of a draw for some of the readers. It is Motorcycles, Mobsters and Mayhem, after all. With his long hair, his cut and aquiline features, he's the epitome of a bad boy. I'm hoping he'll be a similar draw to my table today.

I meant to take advantage of setting up my table last night, which would have been the sensible thing to do, but time and drink had gotten away from me. So now, I've woken up with a myriad of things to do and, as I come to myself, anxious that I won't get it all done on time.

Leaping out of bed, then having to sit down again as the fast movement makes my head swim, I move more gingerly and slowly, shower, and dress myself ready for the day. I've just completed my makeup when a knock sounds at the door.

Having identified StoryTeller and Sheri, I open it.

"You're freaking out." Sheri greets me with a laugh after just one look at my face.

Gesturing at the boxes behind me and the bags of preorders Sheri and I had packed up yesterday, I explain, "I've got to get this lot downstairs and set up…"

"Plenty of time," Sheri interrupts. "We've got a plan for your table, remember? Now you need some food inside you, so come down to breakfast."

My stomach churns at the idea of having anything to eat, but I suppose I need to try.

The gratefulness that I've Sheri and her man to lean on doesn't subside after they've topped me up with coffee, and made me eat some bacon and eggs. It even grows when StoryTeller commandeers a trolley to take all my boxes to the signing room in one go. I'm almost a spare part as Sheri directs StoryTeller on how everything should be placed. Ineffectually, I hand books and swag to her as she sets it all out and then directs StoryTeller to erect my banner and stand it behind the table. Her prior knowledge of signings and organisational skills have really come to my aid.

When I protest I should be doing more, she laughs and tells me I'll be busy enough when the doors open and the readers arrive.

She's even got the preorder bags lined up alphabetically before an announcement comes.

"All authors are to report to the foyer for the group photo."

I feel like I'm in another universe when I go out alongside people whose books I've read and admired for years. Somehow, I end up alongside Winter Travers who has such an amazing way with words. And who I quickly discover is an amazingly kind woman as well, as she helps me position myself so I won't be hidden among the taller authors. Even so, I keep my face slightly averted.

I smile, laugh at the professional photographer's quips designed to get the best pictures, and then return to my table to find my second assistant has arrived.

Helo. Wow, she's striking—tall with short hair. I'm tongue-tied when I go to greet her, but surprisingly, she seems a little nervous as well.

"I've read your books," she tells me, shaking her head and admitting, "I don't normally read fiction, but I loved yours. While you've successfully steered clear of identifying the Soulz, you've really captured their spirit. When's the next one out?"

My cheeks burn at her compliment. Nice comments about my writing are for some reason difficult to take, so I turn the tables on her. "I know your background. I'd love to pick your brains so I can include a Night Stalker in one of my stories."

Her eyes widen. "Really? I'd love that. We'll talk, yeah?"

Oh, so yeah. I'm so caught up in ideas about the type of information I can get from her that I almost miss the announcement that the VIP ticket holders are starting to come in. Sheri's already sitting at the table. I sit in the middle, with Helo on my other side. StoryTeller stands, arms folded behind us like some sexy bodyguard. I rummage in my rucksack for my journal to start picking the Night Stalker's brain and make some notes, when my name, well, J Frobisher, is asked in a nervous, inquisitive voice.

I glance up. "That's me," I confirm, realising any of the three of us could be her. I haven't included my real imagery in any of the publicity. It's still ingrained in me to avoid revealing my face.

"I love your books," the bubbly young woman in front of me says. "I've got a preorder." As she tells us her name, Sheri confidently starts looking through the bags. "Can I take a photo with you?"

I've already noticed it's common practice for the authors to stand posed with their fans and take selfies with them. While the idea of having my face plastered anywhere fills me with concern, I'd look like a bitch if I refused to comply. So, swallowing my worries down, persuading myself that even in the unlikely event Barclay was still looking for me, he's unlikely to search in the social media pages of romance readers.

When I allow her to move me in front of my banner so she gets the full effect, I feel like a rock star as I beam into her phone's camera.

While I'd convinced myself a few photographs probably wouldn't put me in any danger, as I sit down, I come up with a contingency plan. This event will be long over by the time Barclay could come across any photos, and I'll be back living in anonymity by then. *But maybe it will be safer to move out of state.* That wouldn't be a problem. I can write anywhere.

I don't have long to worry about what might happen after the signing as during it I'm much busier than I ever expected. As well as those who've placed preorders, other readers stop when they pass by my table. As expected, StoryTeller is proving a draw. After a worried glance at Sheri, I relax, seeing she's more amused than concerned about the women who are openly flirting with her man. As for him? He's polite but dismissive and rests his hand on her shoulder as if to reassure her he's not going anywhere. I bank little things about their strong relationship in my mental book as it's good background for another novel.

VIP entry over, general admission starts. Now the room really begins to get busy. Lunch comes and goes, and, at last, all my preorders have been collected. There seems to be a lull and my bladder is killing me.

Standing, I tell them, "I need to take a break."

"Going to the heads?" Helo queries. When I nod, she grins. "I'll come along."

I just nod, wondering whether she's got a weak bladder herself, as she's been accompanying Sheri on her hourly breaks.

"You're doing brilliantly," she confides as we exit the room. "You must be so pleased with the amount you've sold."

I'm nearly out of books and there's still an hour or so to go. My stocks of swag have been seriously depleted. "I'm overwhelmed," I reply. "I thought I'd be sitting twiddling my thumbs all day." I grin at her. "And picking your brains about being a Night Stalker."

She snorts. "Hell, you can do that anytime, girl." Her hand touches mine, pausing our forward movement. "Honestly? I really have read your books and you've got talent. I'm more than happy to share what I can of my past if you're truly interested. I know you'd make an amazing story out of it."

I feel the blood rush to my face as I blush. But as I've been trying to ignore my body's urges for the last couple of hours, the need to pee is really becoming urgent. We've started walking again, but I stop short when I see the *closed for maintenance* signs in front of the lady's bathroom. *Shit.*

I feel like I'm in one of my dreams when I'm desperate to go and can never find a facility. I'm looking around for a member of the resort staff to ask where the nearest ones are, when, *thank God,* a man appears and starts removing the signs.

"All yours," he says, grinning. Once more I go red, thinking he can read the desperation on my face.

"Jasmine," Helo says sharply.

I'm literally about to wet myself. Ignoring whatever she's about to say to me, I race inside, go straight into the nearest cubicle, lower my pants and panties and get down to business. Oh, what a relief. I giggle, knowing I mean that literally.

Finishing up, I flush and step outside to wash my hands. I come to a halt when I see Helo held by two men. Her eyes don't need to flash the warning. I immediately know I've fucked up.

There's a third man who's concentrating on me. His lips curve as he smirks. "Your husband awaits you, Katrina."

For some reason, I believe holding my hands, palms forward, and retreating back into the stall is going to save me. Intellectually, I know it won't, but my body's on autopilot. It wouldn't have been safe, but he grabs me before I can reach it in any event.

"You're coming with us." He jerks at my arm.

I'm scared. Terrified. But somehow, I find my voice. I haven't survived three years away from Barclay without growing a spine. "No, I'm not." I say firmly, fighting as hard as I can.

All I do is make him snigger. "Oh, yes, you are."

"What are we going to do about this bitch?" one of the men holding Helo asks. "Shall we kill her?" To demonstrate that they can, another holds a gun pointing straight at her forehead.

I catch my breath. *No, no and no.* Helo didn't get decorated as a hero fighting on foreign soil just to die in a woman's stall on her home turf. I open my mouth to scream she's got nothing to do with me when Thug One, as I've named him, the one holding me, responds, "It will make too much mess if we leave a body. Best disappear as we planned it. Anyway, she could be a bonus. Boss might make some money off her."

"Doubt it," Thug Two answers. "She's got really small tits." He still holds that gun pointed unwaveringly at her.

"But a nice ass," the other states firmly. "That might compensate."

Oh, Helo, what have I gotten you into?

"Let her go," I cry out. "She's nothing to do with me. She was just someone coming into the restroom at the same time."

"Nice try." Thug One smirks. "She's been seated at your table all day. We've been watching you." He inclines his head toward the third thug. "Boris's brother has been working as a janitor which gets him access to all areas." He moves his gaze from me and considers Helo. "Sorry, not sorry, bitch. But you've been inconvenienced just because women have to pee in pairs. Always thought there was something perverted about that. But hey, what do I care? And if the two of you want to make out in front of us, well, you won't hear any complaints." He cackles as though he's made a good joke.

I'm watching Helo carefully, wondering what she's going to do. If it wasn't for the gun, I reckon she'd be showing us how she can handle herself. But even a ninja isn't faster than a bullet. Unlike me, she isn't shaking like a bag of nerves. She's still composed, able to ignore the remarks about her physical appearance, which would make me bristle. Her eyes meet mine briefly, but it's hard to read what she's thinking.

The door to the restroom bursts open, and my heart leaps for a moment until I see it's another man. This one is pushing a large laundry basket. From the familial resemblance, I take it that this is Boris's aforementioned brother.

Before I can take another moment to even think if there's anything I can do to prevent what's coming next, there's a sting in my neck. Slapping my hand on the offending object, I've only time to process a syringe before my vision blurs, I lose control of my muscles, and my world turns black.

CHAPTER THIRTEEN
STRIDER

We've commandeered the assistance of a support club the Soulz have in Dallas and have taken over their clubhouse for the day to act as our headquarters. The weekend warrior fuckers couldn't do enough for us, and seemed overwhelmed to have our one-percenter presence in their home. Not only have they allowed us to house our meetings in their church, but have also instructed their bar to provide us with beers on tap.

Their prez, Rufus, VP, Samba, and SAA, Arch were around to personally welcome us, but they made themselves scarce when we indicated their presence wasn't needed.

Out of respect for the Arizona prez who'd ridden a fair distance to be here, I position a second seat beside mine at the head of the table. Chaz has brought his VP, Bull, sergeant-at-arms, Iron, Weasel, his road captain, and Claws, his enforcer with him. I've got Shotgun, Tequila, Buzz, Madman, Shout and Tex here. Drumming my fingers against the table, I impatiently wait for Data and Legend, my IT expert, and Chaz's to join us.

Chaz grins at me, his bald head shining in the harsh overhead lights. "Club prez here seems a pussy."

I shrug. "They're an okay support club. Keep themselves to themselves, mind their own business, follow the rules, and give assistance where needed. What more could I ask?"

He rolls his eyes. "Ever met Drummer of the Satan's Devils?"

I smirk. "Heard of them. Now they're made of different stuff. The real shit."

He nods slowly. "Men you'd want on your side, not against you."

I raise my chin to acknowledge his point. This club is welcoming, but if hell broke out, we couldn't depend on them to stand beside us.

Being the dominant club, the Wretched Soulz vet all MCs setting up on our territory. This one's harmless enough, pay their dues on time, and give us respect. But he's got a point. I've only met the man at some of the ride-outs our joint clubs join, but my impression of Drummer is sound. He's one motherfucker I'd like on my side in a time like this.

Chaz casts his eyes to the door, seemingly as anxious as I am to get an update. He confirms it when he states, "My woman's in that fuckin' signing."

Bull snorts. "She can look after herself."

Chaz sends him a glare. "More worried about the cleanup she'll leave for us if any trouble starts."

"Cleans up after herself." Claws chuckles, completely unconcerned.

I've met Helo at the Arizona clubhouse, and hell, I've got to admire Chaz for taking her on. She's something else. I'm pleased as fuck to know she's currently sitting beside my woman. With StoryTeller and the Night Stalker, Jasmine's got more than enough protection. Or that's what I use to console myself.

At last, the door opens. Legend's first to enter, Data not far behind. Both geeks take the two empty chairs, and I'm not sure I like the grins they give each other.

With no gavel, I slam my fist on the table. "Update," I demand.

Data sits back in his chair and links his hands behind his head. He glances around lazily, then announces, "Ain't got anything to worry about, Prez. Barclay Aster is not going to put in an appearance. He's," he makes air quotes with his fingers, "otherwise engaged."

Legend butts in, "Yeah, as we speak, he's up in front of a judge discussing his unpaid taxes."

What? "You've confirmed he's there?" I snap, sitting forward.

Data nods then follows up his gesture with, "Yeah. He sure is."

Mex chuckles loudly. "He going down?"

"Fuck no," Legend answers, lines on his forehead. "Judge is a golfing partner of his lawyer. Case is a formality and sure to be dismissed. But all that matters is that he can't be in two places at once, so Strider," he nods to me, and I raise my chin back, "your woman's safe."

It should be good news. I should be delighted. But the hairs rise on the back of my neck, and something in my gut tells me things aren't right.

Madman sighs and leans back in his seat. "I was enjoying the hospitality here, but I suppose we're riding back to Austin and that our friends from AZ have had a wasted journey."

Chaz turns a presidential glare toward him that would match one of my own. "No one's going anywhere until our women are back safe and sound." He bangs his hand down. "Not leaving without my Queenie."

Shotgun turns to face me. "And you're going to want to talk to Jasmine. Persuade her to come home." He, too, frowns Madman's way. "So we're here until the end of the day. We'll pick them up at the end of the signing."

Madman doesn't look contrite. He rolls his eyes, then asks, "Well, can we get more of the free beers in here then?"

As long as they stay relatively sober, I don't mind. I beckon to Mex to go make arrangements. Rufus, it seems, can't do enough for us, and within moments, not only have we each got a fresh round, but plates of delicacies appear before us. Apparently, Arch's old lady's a quite renowned baker, a talent we benefit from.

With no immediate enemy and nothing to plan, our two charters start chatting among ourselves.

"Sorry about Anna." Chaz leans toward me. "You were a fuckin' saint looking after her all this time." I narrow my eyes at him. He's one of the few people who know what happened that far back in time. But there's no shutting him up. "Wasn't your fault, Strider." It doesn't matter who tells me, but no one will ever know the truth of the matter. He reads that in my eyes. "You couldn't have done more for her."

I tried. Even a God I don't believe in must know I tried.

"You deserve something good in your life," he continues. "I like Jasmine for you."

Fuck, so do I. Haven't I done my penance?

I angle my body toward him and say confidentially, "I just hope she'll give me a chance."

He looks at me intently. "Tell her the truth, Brother. The *whole* truth."

Maybe he's right. I take a moment to pick up one of the

delicious doughnuts and take a bite. My phone rings. Swallowing my mouthful down, I answer.

"ST."

"Chaz there?"

"Yeah."

"Put me on speaker."

I do. His tone makes me almost choke on the morsel that feels like it's got stuck in my throat.

StoryTeller wastes no time. "Jasmine went to the restroom and Helo went with her. They were gone too long, so I went to look for them. There was an 'out of order' sign outside. Realising they might have gone some way to find a different one, I wasn't too worried."

"No fuckin' time for one of your stories now, ST," Chaz growls. "Get to the point."

"Then a resort employee comes rushing up, swearing about clowns putting out signs. The rest room was fine. I went in. There was no one inside."

"They might have been fooled and gone to another bathroom." I'm clutching at straws.

StoryTeller's growl comes clearly across the line. "I'd bank everything I own on this being a setup. Don't think we should waste time."

Chaz, like me, is clearly worried but exploring all avenues. "Any sign of a struggle?"

Why hadn't I thought to ask that? Jasmine wouldn't go quietly, and as for Helo, well, single-handed she could take any number of men down.

But we're disavowed of that immediately as StoryTeller replies drily, "Discarded hypodermics in the trash."

"We're on it!" Legend calls out from the opposite end of the table, pointing between Data and himself. Their laptops are open in front of them and Data's fingers are moving fast. "We're trying to get into the CCTV from the resort."

I want to tell them to move faster, but from the expressions on their faces, I bite my tongue. Frustration is written all over them.

"What do you want me to do?" StoryTeller asks. *Fuck knows.* Apart from finding my girl. "There's security here—"

"Whoever's taken them won't be hanging around," Chaz barks. "Good money on that they've already left the resort. Best to get no one else involved. There's nothing they can do that Soulz can't."

"Okay," StoryTeller drawls as if he's thinking. "The event's not far from over, so Sheri and I can pack up her stuff. Make some excuse she's not feeling well."

I wonder whether that's the best option. My gut screams I want everyone looking out for her. But logically, I know she will be nowhere in the building and already off the resort grounds. The only good thing is if they just wanted to kill her, they'd have done so in the restroom and then got out.

She's still alive. That's the only thing I can hang onto.

Chaz grunts out approval for StoryTeller's plan, then reaches over and ends the call. He's just opening his mouth when Legend yells, "Fuck yeah!" and fist-pumps his hand.

Data gives the explanation. "We couldn't get in, but we messaged Mayhem. He's in and is sharing the footage now."

Brothers start getting to their feet, but Buzz shouts out, "Everyone, sit the fuck down." He raises his chin toward Chaz and me, showing that he knows our women are missing and that we want to see the footage without being crowded out.

Rising, I go one way around the table while my Arizonan counterpart goes the other. In similar poses with folded arms, we watch the footage from various angles, covering all the exits.

My fingernails curl into my palms as time seems to fly by with nothing to see. Not that we're really certain what we're looking for. Surely, they won't be so obvious as to carry two unconscious women outside.

"There!" Data points at the screen. He runs it back, then forward again in slow motion.

I see it now. A hotel laundry basket appears at an exit. As it comes more fully into view, there's only one man dressed as a janitor nonchalantly wheeling it out, and while there's no sound, I'd swear he was whistling to himself.

Legend taps away, and on his screen he's following the cameras. When the man on Data's screen disappears out of range, Legend already has him appearing on the other. Data's about to switch the views, but Chaz stops him.

As I focus on where the laundry basket is heading, Chaz continues to stare at the empty exit.

"Yeah!" he exclaims. "Get as good images as you can."

My attention caught, I glance over. There are three other men who do not look like they'd be attending a book signing, and they're keeping their distance but definitely following the cart.

The janitor reaches a white van. This was obviously planned as he pulls out a ramp. When the others catch up with him, they help him push the cart up and inside the van.

"Get the fuckin' license plate," I growl, unable to stay quiet, though I know my brothers will already be on top of anything I could think of.

Data reads a message that flicks up on his screen. "Mayhem's tracking them through traffic cameras."

"Why not get StoryTeller to follow them?" Madman calls out.

Legend points to the timestamp on the screen. "We're not

watching this in real-time. They were already close to the van when he first called us. They're long gone now."

It's something I'd forgotten myself, but I quickly catch up. "Where are they now?"

"Heading north," Legend informs me.

"Brothers!" My loud shout has everyone's attention. "Get ready to ride."

CHAPTER FOURTEEN
JASMINE

Coming to, I find my hands tied painfully behind me, thin plastic digging into my skin. The soreness of my wrists is competing with the pounding in my head. Focusing my eyes, I see Helo looking far more awake than me and brighter than she should be as she shakes out her free hands.

"How did...?" Surely they tied her just as tight as me.

She snorts softly. "It was one of our regular pastimes in the Night Stalkers. Who could get out of zip ties the fastest." As I redouble my efforts, she shakes her head. "No, you'll hurt yourself. You have to be prepared from the start and tense your muscles just so when they put them on. I'll get yours off you in a moment."

Still feeling woozy, wondering how she could have shaken the effects of whatever they'd injected us with so fast, I can only watch as she stealthily moves around what appears to be some kind of basement they've imprisoned us in. There's a chest of drawers that she goes through, tutting when she can find nothing to help. I hear a smashing, see her tense, turn, and regard the door, then relax when no sound can be heard.

She comes over to me. "Got a piece of glass that should work."

I don't even grunt when a jagged edge cuts into me. I just want my hands untied *now*. I let out a gasp of relief as the hard plastic binding my wrists falls away.

"Sorry I nicked you."

Shrugging, I tell her, "You got me free." I see her grinning, and ask, "What?"

"You're a real prez's old lady, aren't you?"

Vigorously, I shake my head. "I'm nothing to Strider." I try, but I can't say the words he's nothing to me.

She cocks her head strangely, but whatever she's about to say remains unsaid as footsteps sound. Flinging herself to the position I first saw her in, she pulls her hands behind her back. As she beckons to me, I do the same.

The door opens. I catch my breath as a man all too familiar comes into sight. *No, this can't be happening again.*

Ignoring Helo, the man stops in front of me. While waiting for him to say something, I notice another man, heavily armed, standing just inside the door. "Katrina," he purrs. "We meet again. I can't wait until we can get properly reacquainted."

He's one of Barclay's minions who raped me time and time again, never caring how much he hurt me. I try to keep hold of my sanity, from drowning in despair, fighting to think rationally. *He said he can't wait.* In the past, he'd just take what he wanted. There must be a reason he's not reaching for me immediately.

Trying to put strength into my voice, I ask, "Where's Barclay?"

He snorts. "He wanted to be here to greet you, but he had another prior meeting he couldn't get out of. Don't worry. He'll be here as soon as he can. And I, for one, can't wait to see your reunion." He gets closer, so near I can smell his fetid breath, and my stomach churns, remembering the feeling of him on top of me. "You've been a fucking naughty girl, but the boss is aware of your tricks now. You're going to get what's coming. I know how much he's been looking forward to this."

I really hope I can't guess what he's talking about, but I take some comfort that Barclay's not here right now, and I've got time. What this raping brute doesn't know is that both Helo's and my hands are unbound and that my companion herself is my secret weapon. Maybe I'm building up her skills in my mind, but I think she's more than a match for them, well, as long as she's not looking down the barrel of a gun.

He's still smirking. "I'll just leave you… ladies… to yourselves. Barclay will be here in the morning." He turns and goes, followed by the guard. It's impossible not to hear the key in the lock turning.

My strength leaves me, and I curl into myself, unable to stop shaking. My nightmare has come true. I've fucked up and now Barclay's found me.

"Stop panicking, woman," Helo snaps a few seconds after the door closes. "The Wretched Soulz will be looking for us. And even if they don't find us, we're not poor defenceless women."

Speak for yourself. I might have grown in confidence with Strider wanting me exclusively and giving me some position in the clubhouse, but now, faced with my past, I'm back to the feeble woman controlled by her husband and in abject terror at the thought of seeing him again.

She speaks patiently, as though to a child. "There are weapons here. We've just got to find them."

I'm out of my depth, but as Helo stands and starts moving around, kicking the hell out of one of the drawers and triumphantly holding up a dangerous-looking piece of wood when she's finished, I start to catch on.

Standing, telling myself I'd rather die fighting than let Barclay put his hands on me again, I, too, start to look at my surroundings, trying to see as though I was looking through Helo's eyes. I find a shard from the glass she'd broken earlier, and while I'm not sure if I could stab another human being, I harden myself, knowing I would do anything to stop myself from being raped again.

After a while, we've gathered and hidden a few weapons we could use, and I'm feeling stronger. Thank fuck she's here with me. I'd be nothing if I was here by myself.

I don't know what time it is. It had been around three in the afternoon when we were taken, but how long the drugs kept us out is hard to estimate. We've got all night until Barclay makes an appearance, but there's no way I'm going to be able to sleep.

Helo leans up against the wall and regards me in the dim light from the small bulb that's been left glowing.

"Do you know the full story about Strider's wife?"

Grimacing, I reply, "Yeah. She's the love of his life who he's having to watch slowly die."

"And you know she never wanted to have anything to do with the biker life?"

I nod my reply.

"Chaz and Strider were close from way back in the day," she begins. "Strider found in Chaz someone he could confide in, talk to him about shit that even his closest brothers didn't know." She glances at me to see if I'm paying attention. "Childhood sweethearts don't always make great partners for life, and sometimes they develop different wants and needs. Even before Strider got out of the service and joined the club, he was addicted to motorcycles. Anna wanted nothing to do with it."

"He's told me that," I interrupt.

She raises and dips her chin. "But have you thought what him joining the club really meant? He put his wants and needs above his love for her. Does that tell you anything about the state of their relationship at the time?"

"Anna could already have been ill and acting out of character."

"They married directly from high school, and then Strider was away for eight years being a Marine. I've seen it time and time again in the service. Marriage quite often doesn't survive, especially when kids who marry young mature into adults." She glances to see if I'm taking it all in. "Strider was about to divorce her when he realised things were wrong." She pauses, swallows, her brow furrows and she shakes her head. "During the diagnosis, he asked the question and got the answer that a TBI, traumatic brain injury, could be the cause of Picks Disease. From that moment on, he decided the accident he'd had the one and only time she went on his bike was the reason why she got ill and became consumed with guilt."

"Do you think he's right?"

Helo shrugs. "Who knows? There's much the doctors don't know about how the brain works. She could have been born with the time bomb already inside her head, or, yes, it could have been the injury when she fell off the bike. Whatever. Strider felt such guilt that he might have caused what happened to her that he took it upon himself to always be there for her. But that's not the same thing as love. You hearing me now?"

I'm hearing her. I'm listening. I still believe, though, that Strider's actions seemed to say something different. "He took me to see her. To show me why we could never be a thing."

"He took you to see her, to show you how he, too, was suffering. And needed you to wait for him."

Shaking my head, I tell her, "I'm not hanging around until his beloved wife dies, and then play second fiddle."

For a moment, her eyes simply focus on mine, and then she tells me, "Firstly, Anna died a couple of weeks back. And secondly, you're no substitute. From the way Strider's been in pieces since he couldn't find out where you'd gone, shows he's a man who's fucking head and tails in love. With you. Not her."

Anna's dead?

I've been taking it on trust that she's only here because she read my books and enjoyed them. I narrow my eyes. She seems to know a lot about Strider and what he's been like since I left. "Just why did you want to come to the signing?"

I think she can see by my expression that I'm not going to accept any half-truths or lies. As the corners of her lips curve upward, she says, "Strider's been searching for you. He knows exactly who you are. And *he still wants you.*"

My jaw drops. How could he? I never gave him any clue to suggest I wasn't Jasmine Smart. Shaking my head, I refute it. "He can't know." My voice is just a whisper.

She grins. "He knows you're Katrina Aster and that you're still married. It did take a while to find out the details, but the essence you told him yourself. You wrote it all down."

I bang the heel of my hand against my forehead. I've known Strider had read my book and realised I'd written about him, as prez, me as the club girl, and the relationship I'd always dreamed of. As for the rest of the story, I'd thought it so incredible that no one would believe there was any truth behind it.

"He's been so worried," she continues. "That's why I thought I'd volunteer to be part of your protection. Which is why I'm here now." She glances down, then up at me again. "Chaz counts him among his closest friends, and fate hasn't treated him kindly."

"Whoa. Back up a moment. Protection? Why did anyone think I needed protection?"

Patiently, as though speaking to a child, she explains, "Because if the Soulz could find out you're really Katrina Aster née James, then Barclay with all of his connections would likewise know where to find you." She pauses, then says with emphasis, "At the signing you decided to attend."

Lowering my head into my hands, I realise I really haven't been as clever as I thought I was. "I used my grandmother's maiden name."

Raising her chin, she agrees, "That was the key to finding you."

I shake my head and say with feeling, "Shit." Then I realise while this kidnapping had come to me as a complete surprise, my companion had come along today knowing the risk something like this was going to happen. "I don't know why you would put yourself in danger if you knew there was a chance Barclay had found out where I'd be and come for me. What the fuck were you thinking?"

She bristles now. "Girl, do you hear what you just said to me?"

"You could have been killed!"

"I could have died many times before, but I haven't. You're important to Strider, which means you're important to all the Soulz. There was no point putting a brother on you. They'd have been killed, not brought along. But a woman? Yeah, Barclay's played right into my hands. As soon as they saw another female, they wanted me. Even with my small tits," she ends with a laugh.

I burst into a chuckle. "But a fine ass."

She does a body shimmer and giggles. "A girl's got to work with whatever she has."

Soberness comes over me. "I still can't understand why Chaz would put you in danger."

"Chaz doesn't 'put' me in anything. And facing someone like your ex is child's play, considering all the other risks I've taken." Grimacing slightly, she admits, "And then I let my guard down. Just before you needed that comfort break, I got a text saying Barclay was out of the picture, in front of a judge. So I stupidly thought it was unlikely he'd try anything."

Again, my mouth drops open. Hope floods into me. Has the legal system really caught up with him? "Will he go down?"

She throws cold water on that immediately and rolls her eyes. "Unlikely. He's got good connections to the judge."

"I'm sorry." Suddenly, the words flow out of me. "You shouldn't be here. This is all on me, on my head. I should never have thought I'd have anonymity while attending the signing." Rubbing my hands over my face, I continue, "I was so damn stupid. I let the success of my books run away with me."

Helo approaches, her features set. "Jasmine. You've built yourself an incredible career. I'm not a reader, but the minute I picked up your first book, I was truly drawn into it. It's Barclay who's got no right to interfere. And it's him who's going down."

Her fierceness and the forceful delivery of her words start me thinking that maybe there's a way to get out of this. I'm terrified, yes. Dreading seeing Barclay again, but I'm not alone, and there's no one else I'd rather have beside me.

Except for the whole charter of the Wretched Soulz, of course.

If I'd been alone, I'd be going crazy. "Why did you let yourself get captured along with me? Couldn't you have gotten away yourself?"

Helo sits on the floor beside me, lays back, and puts her hands behind her head. "I had a split second to make a decision. Yeah, I could have disarmed that man easily, but there was a risk that there were more of them outside. If they saw me as a threat, they could have disposed of me and taken you. Thought you had more of a chance if I stuck with you." She's certainly not wrong there. She changes the subject. "Reckon we should try to get some rest. I estimate it's around midnight, and we've got a few hours before Barclay's likely to make it here."

I suppose she's got a point. I've still got a dull headache from whatever drug I was given. Beneath my ass, the floor is cold, hard and unyielding, but dutifully, copying my companion, I lie myself down and then sit back up. Helo seems as relaxed as though she was lying on a five-star mattress.

At my restlessness, Helo opens her eyes and raises her brow quizzically.

"The floor's too hard."

She snorts. "Believe me, it's luxury compared to some of the places I've slept in. I was held hostage for six months. The ground I slept on was rocky desert."

My hand covers my mouth.

Her face softens. "I, too, was raped. We've got more in common than you think, Jasmine." Her tone becomes firmer. "And we both survived."

Personally, I don't think there's too much common ground between us. She's a real-life hero for a start. Her approach to our situation makes me feel ashamed. So as she lies back down, I do likewise, curling myself into a fetal position, trying to make belief I'm lying on something soft rather than this hard ground.

I try not to toss and turn so as not to disturb her, and at some point, I must fall asleep.

I'm woken abruptly by a sound at the door. First thing I notice is that Helo's woken before me and has taken position standing by the entrance to the basement. She's unarmed, as far as I can tell.

Footsteps sound. Helo hisses, "Put your hands behind your back."

I've only a moment to do as she says when the door creaks open, and I freeze. It's been three years since I last saw my husband, and I hoped I'd never see him again. I'd become too complacent, thinking he was a distant memory. But here he is now, and my first inclination is to vomit.

He saunters into the basement as if he owns the place, which he probably does. Only one guard accompanies him. Well, why would he need more? I've never put up a fight in my life, despite the times he'd hurt me. I now wonder why I'd been so compliant. If I'd fought back, I'd have died. But might that have been better than letting his men use me?

I'm not going back. I'm not going to do that again. I won't let my father's sacrifice be in vain.

I realise my heart's pounding and I'm breathing too fast when Helo says softly, "Relax, Jasmine."

Barclay stops in front of me. He spares a quick glance at my companion standing by the door, looking like her hands are still bound behind her, then dismisses her and returns his attention to me. He stares at me for a moment, looking me up and down, then sneers. "Christ, you've let yourself go."

I'm dressed as an author who writes MC romance—a tee shirt with a Harley on it, jeans and boots. I thought I looked cute, though, obviously not to him.

"And you're just a picture of health," I snarkily respond, knowing I shouldn't anger him but wanting to point out that he's not exactly a catch with his alcohol-flushed cheeks and red-rimmed eyes.

My response gets a sharp kick to my leg, and it takes all I

have to keep my hands clasped behind me and only do so as I've locked my fingers together.

"You have no idea how much I hate you. Always hated you, in fact. There's nothing about you that redeems the woman you are. You're an ugly bitch." He pauses and waits for a reaction, but I give him none. Words are just that and can't hurt me. If he thinks I'll be offended by his summation of me, then he's wrong. I don't give a damn. He sucks in a breath and suddenly screams at me. "You were always useless." He spits at me now, and I only just manage to turn my face in time. "You couldn't even give me a kid."

"Maybe it wasn't me who was lacking." I shouldn't enrage him. I've never stood up to him before. But somehow, knowing Helo's a hero makes me want to be strong.

He rears back. "I've gotten women pregnant," he snarls.

Oh yeah, only a monster would be proud of that. "Then you don't need me to produce an heir."

He gives a skeletal grin. "But they weren't *my wife*. They either got rid of it or died." He regards me for a moment. "But you're right. I can find a more suitable woman to continue my bloodline. I don't need you pregnant or even alive. It's far better for me if you're dead. I'll get your inheritance left by your dear old dad."

His manner of speaking is chilling, but knowing how wrong he is, I can't help but snort. "My father had no money. He couldn't give you more when he died."

Barclay smiles that demonic smile again. "Have you never heard the term asset rich, cash poor?" For a moment, he almost looks sympathetic. "He had nothing to give me while he was alive, but what he left to you were all his buildings and businesses. More than enough to cover his debt." Now he's back to sneering. "You're a rich woman, and you don't even realise it.

You spend your life whoring yourself out to bikers and writing smut to survive."

"It's not smut," I snarl while realising that's the least of things that should concern me.

He pinches the brow of his nose, looks like he's thinking for a moment, then cheerily says, "I'll be doing you a favour, letting you do some research. May even get new material." His mirth disappears. "Such a shame you won't be able to use it, but my men will enjoy fucking the life out of you. Take a good look around, as this is going to be the last place you'll ever see."

I take a step back. I knew what fate was in store for me as soon as my *husband* appeared, but I thought I'd have time, maybe even escape again, or have time so that the Wretched Soulz would come looking for us. Even if Strider doesn't care about me, Chaz will come for Helo. *Should I plead, beg for time, throw myself on his mercy?* But he had none for me last time. And to him, money is worth far more than me.

He sneers at the distress that must be showing on my face, then moves his attention to Helo. "Didn't expect any collateral benefits from reclaiming my wife. You? You're definitely lacking in some areas, but I'm sure to find a market for you somewhere. I suspect my men would like to try you out."

Helo's completely still. She doesn't so much as flinch at his appraisal. Her non-reaction catches him unaware.

"Come here," he barks. "Let me get a good look at you."

Helo had stayed quiet while he was berating me, but she'd obviously been summing him up. I could have told her Barclay always goes unarmed, letting others do his dirty work for him, but she's obviously worked that out for herself. She obediently moves forward awkwardly, with her hands still held behind her back. But once close enough, she stops the pretence and turns into a whirling dervish of arms, legs and body, throwing herself at his bodyguard. The man is unarmed and unconscious before I can blink. And Barclay? Well, she's got him held tight and captive before he can scream, with her hand over his mouth.

"You want to go through a divorce or want me to take care of him now?"

I don't want to breathe the same air. I swallow a couple of times, wondering whether this woman is really me. Then realise I'd become hardened when my father took his life in front of me. If Barclay had been someone different, someone kind and caring as Dad originally thought he would be, I'd still have one parent alive. Barclay deserves no mercy from me. "Take care of him."

The speed in which she twists his neck, killing him without second thought, startles me. But I've no emotion other than elation when the man who tortured me, who promised me more suffering, falls dead at my feet.

She's totally unemotional when she turns to me. "Now, we've got to get out of here."

But Barclay's dead. Surely my nightmare is over? I'm now a free woman.

My brain rattles in my head as she shakes me. "Come on, Jasmine. Barclay's got men upstairs. You think they won't want to avenge his death and get some compensation for the loss of their pay ticket and boss?"

Her actions and words bring me to my senses.

We might have felled a major tree, but we're certainly not out of the woods yet. I swallow, straighten my back, and get ready to fight.

CHAPTER FIFTEEN
STRIDER

"Where the fuck are they?" I repeat again. Memories slam into my head, pictures of past events flashing through my mind. The accident which left Anna with a concussion, the guilt I'd felt at the time, magnified a hundred fold when she'd gotten her diagnosis. The acceptance, now, that our marriage wouldn't have stood the test of time if I hadn't felt so damn responsible for her. And, the realisation, I'd done the best that I could. That I owed nothing further to her.

If I'd been the one to go first, I wouldn't have wanted Anna to waste the rest of her life, to live lonely and alone, mourning lost opportunities. I'd be doing her a disservice to think she'd not feel the same way.

Thinking back, my Anna, the one I fell in love with, wouldn't have wanted me to waste time.

She'd have liked Jasmine. If she'd allowed herself to have a relationship with the club, I could have seen them being friends. And, of course, she used to read the same books as Jasmine writes.

I can have Jasmine and still honour Anna's memory.

But I've got to find her and rescue her first.

The phone rings. Chaz, obviously going through the same version of hell, reaches for it, but I get there first, putting it immediately on speaker.

"Mayhem here," the voice of our Californian member sounds. Without preamble, he enlightens us. "The van disappeared into an underground parking lot..."

"Where?" I interrupt. "We're ready to go now." I raise my hand to tee up my men.

"Hold your fuckin' horses. There'd be no point. It's under a bank. Most likely, they've changed vehicles now."

Chaz's face is thunderous. "We've fuckin' lost them?"

Mayhem sounds unperturbed. "Trying a different tactic. Looking into businesses Barclay owns and those he's associated with. Got a few of locations..."

"Give us them," I demand. "We'll check them out."

Patiently, Mayhem waits while Chaz demands the same thing, only using a few different words, and then again, calmly states, "As expected, Barclay had all charges against him dismissed. He's a free man. Well, except for the tracker that I got someone at the courthouse to put on him. He's going to lead us to the women. You've just got to be patient and ready to ride once we know where he's headed."

Raking my hands through my hair, I glare at the phone. "He let his goons rape her before. What's the difference now? She's worth more to him dead than alive." My fist hits the table. "We've got no fuckin' time to spare. We've got to get to her before he does."

Chaz's hand covers mine. "Brother, I fuckin' hear you. My Queenie's involved as well. The risk is worse for her. She's nothing to Barclay except for another female body they might be able to profit from. Don't you think I'm going mad here, thinking of what might be happening to her?"

Shrugging him off, I snarl, "Then you see my point. We can't sit here doing nothing."

"Then what the fuck do you think we should be doing?" Shotgun suddenly roars. "Prez, I hear you. All of us are worried sick about what's happening to Jasmine and Helo right now. But if we split ourselves thin, tear off in different directions, we might miss our chance completely or not be in the right place when they need us around."

"Jasmine's resilient," Tequila backs him up. "She's a survivor. She's gotten through what a lot of women couldn't before. Mayhem's plan gives us the best fuckin' chance of rescuing her."

"They might be hurting her," I roar, standing so fast my chair flies over.

Shaking his head, Shotgun moves behind me, rights it, and squeezes his fingers on my shoulder. "If she's hurt, then you, *we*, can put her back together. If she's dead..." His voice trails off, but he's made his point.

Standing, Chaz clasps me to him, slapping one hand against my back. He releases me fast, and when I look into his eyes, I see my own pain mirrored.

"Queenie's collateral damage," he states. "She's in even more danger than your woman. But I've got to take heart in the fact they can't know who they've taken. My Queenie, my Helo, she'll do all she can to survive and make sure both she and Jasmine get out alive. Ain't no other outcome I can bear thinking about." He pauses and glances at Shotgun as if he wants third-party confirmation. "From what I'm hearing, Jasmine isn't going to simply fold. She's going to fight with everything she's got. We've got to have faith in our women and stay here until we've got better information and know exactly where to target our help."

"Barclay's private plane has just taken off. Flight plan filed says he's coming to Dallas," Mayhem, still on the phone, informs us.

Mex hollers, "Then let's get to the airfield and head him off."

"Can't do that," Buzz patiently replies. "His men have already got Jasmine, and what are they likely to do without their boss?"

Rape her. If they haven't already.

Mayhem's voice again comes through the speaker. "I'm tracking him, remember? Once he's landed and I've got a direction he's headed, I can match that with the locations I've identified."

It's a plan. Raising my chin toward Chaz, I take my seat once more. Gut churning, I want to leap into action, but I have to accept I can't do anything now. "How long until his plane lands?"

"Two hours," Mayhem answers fast as if he'd predicted I would ask. "Then he'll need time to get through the airport."

"Keep us up to date." I end the call, knowing there's no point in Mayhem hanging around for the time Aster is in the air.

"Er," someone tentatively starts. Raising my eyes, I see it's Chaz's enforcer who's sounding unusually mild. "You think they've got any more food around here?"

"Good fuckin' plan," Madman says.

Closing my eyes, I try hard to pull myself back into my president's shoes. I might be Jasmine's man, even if she doesn't yet understand, but rant and rave as much as I like, I've got to be patient. An army fights on its stomach, so fuelling our bodies is a good idea. Not that I, personally, think I can force anything down.

Madman slips out and manages to find Samba, who gets their prospects in line. Soon, the table is covered in a choice of bacon or burger sandwiches, pots of coffee and cups abound, along with a selection of beer bottles, but most of us opt for caffeine, wanting to keep sharp heads about us.

Rather than staying seated, like others, I stand. Shotgun's propped himself against the wall, and I pace around. After a moment, he pushes away and comes to stand by my side.

"Not eating anything, Prez?" He glances at the lone cup of coffee in my otherwise empty hands.

I let him in on what's going around my head. "If we hadn't gotten our wires crossed…" I swallow and start again. "I only meant to show her my prior commitment. I didn't mean to chase her away."

"Fuck that." He glares at me. "Don't put this all upon yourself, Prez. You got some kind of God complex? You think everything's your fault? You've taken the guilt of Anna's condition all on your head when there was no proof to substantiate it. You're not responsible or in control of everything Fate deals out. Anna could have always had her illness waiting in the background, and as for Jasmine? She'd have attended this signing whether she was with the Soulz or not. Barclay would still have been able to find her." Pausing, he beckons Buzz over. "Knock some sense into him, will you?"

I'd like to avoid Buzz's meaty fists and look down suspiciously, primed to react if there's any sign he's taking the VP's words literally.

But as Shotgun walks away, my sergeant-at-arms just looks at me sadly. "What happened to Anna wasn't your fault. It might have been nothing to do with the bike accident. If it was an injury, she might have been dropped on her head as a baby, for all that you know. At the end of the day, it was more likely the bad luck of the draw that she had some faulty genetics. And Jasmine? Well, she should have trusted us." He shrugs and harrumphs. "Maybe not from the start when she first came to us, but once you laid claim to her..." he waves me down as I open my mouth to refute I ever did that. "Sure, you didn't come out and say it, but making her off-limits to anyone else? Sure sent a strong message. We treated her like a sister. That day? When she left the club? We all begged her to stay."

"Why did she leave when she knew she had trouble waiting for her?"

Buzz sighs heavily. "She's the only one who can answer that. But my best guess is, after three years, reckon she thought, or hoped, she'd be safe, and..." he reminds me. "It wasn't exactly easy to find her."

Nodding slowly, I have to admit she was right. If it hadn't been for her books, for this damn signing, neither I nor Aster would ever have been able to find her. Much as I want the feel of her in my arms again, I'd give that up in a moment if it meant no one else could touch her.

Now all I can do is wait. I take out my phone and check the time again. It's still another sixty minutes until Aster's plane will land. As soon as he does, Mayhem will again be able to start tracking.

I visit the heads, not out of necessity, but to ensure I'm ready to ride and nothing will cause any delay. I notice several brothers have left the room, and from the coming and going of engine sounds outside, decide that, sensibly, they're topping off their bikes. I'd had to get gas shortly before I arrived, so that's one task that's already done and dusted.

I take out my gun, check both the weapon itself and the ammunition I carry, and then do the same to the spare in my ankle holster. Around me, brothers who ride with me, and those who are with Chaz, are also making sure they're prepared. The coffee has gone, and most of the beers remain. Every man is taking this seriously.

Legend whoops. "Mayhem's got the location. Aster's definitely headed in the location of one of the premises Mayhem previously identified." He raises his eyes and focuses on Chaz. "We've got this, Prez."

Data, acknowledging me, confirms, "I'm sending the location to all your phones now."

"Brothers!" I holler, thumping my fist down. "We go in quiet. We don't know what we're facing, how many, or who might be there. Wet work if possible, bullets the last resort, and... Barclay Aster is fuckin' mine."

Chaz is staring at a laptop Legend's turned toward him. "Main entrance, two exits. No idea where the women are being held." He glances at me, and while he makes a statement, his brows rise, making it a question. "Strider leads half his men and takes the main entrance. I'll go in with mine and the exit here at the back."

"Shotgun will take the others to the side door," I finish for him. There's only one thing left to say. "Let's fuckin' ride."

CHAPTER SIXTEEN

JASMINE

"Can you fire a gun?"

That's one skill I have got, so confidently, I reply to Helo, "Yeah, Buzz and Shotgun took me out to their range a few times."

She's frisked the unconscious guard and passes his weapon over to me.

"Er," I hesitate. "Wouldn't it be better if you took this?"

She grins and barks a short laugh. "As long as you can hit a big-ass target, then no. I'm better with this." She holds up an evil-looking knife. "And my bare hands. Unless you're a jujitsu expert and haven't told me."

Despite the circumstances, never mind that my husband's dead body is at my feet, I have to smile. "Nah, I've no hidden talents."

"Then let's get ourselves out." She holds out her fist and I bump it with mine.

But as I look at the door and remember at least one of my previous rapists is somewhere behind it, my nerves show themselves. "Helo?" I can't rid the panic from my tone.

"Shouldn't we just wait here? Chaz will be looking for you." And if she's right about Strider, he will be too.

With only a slight indrawn and exhaled breath to reveal she's sighed, she replies patiently, "I'm sure that the Soulz are moving heaven and earth trying to find us. But there's no guarantee they're going to discover where we are. We're not going to stay undisturbed for ever. Sooner or later, someone will come down, or sleeping beauty there will wake up." She jerks her head toward the unconscious body on the ground. "Unless you want me to silence him permanently, we need to act now while we've got the element of surprise."

I've astounded myself with my lack of compassion for Barclay's demise, relief being my foremost emotion. And though I doubt the man who accompanied him has less evil intentions than him, I'm squeamish and don't want to witness him being killed in cold blood.

Helo's obviously preparing to leave and goes toward the stairs. Not wanting to be left behind, I follow her up. Slowly and quietly, she opens the door. It leads to a small hallway that has been left unguarded. We both step through, then she turns and locks the door behind us.

Voices reach us from somewhere. Her finger to her mouth, Helo beckons me to be quiet. She appears to be listening, I suppose, to precisely locate where they are, and how many there are of them.

When I start to pick out the words they're saying, bile rises in my throat. They're talking about me and her and all of the perverted things they'd like to do to us. As I inhale sharply, Helo's hand reaches out and squeezes mine, a sign of solidarity. The stiffening of her body suggests she's not unaffected.

She holds up three fingers and raises a quizzical brow. Trying to divorce myself from the sentiment and count up the different tones, I nod, confirming that I think she's right. Her brief nod of reassurance and quick quirk of her lips implies she's okay with those odds.

Gripping the pistol more firmly, checking the safety is off, I brace myself. I've never considered myself a fighter. Barclay's death has opened up a new world of freedom in front of me, completing the process for which my father had sacrificed his life. I'm determined to do everything I can not to waste the chance I've been given.

Footsteps sound and a voice calls out, close enough we can hear the words clearly. "I'll check on the boss. Thought I'd be hearing screams by now." His mirthful tone sends shivers down my spine.

"You just wanna join in," another shouts.

Helo stealthily moves to position herself before the turn in the hallway. A man appears. He sees me, but before he can do anything more than open his mouth, his throat is cut and he's bleeding out on the floor.

I suppose Helo used hand signals in her previous employment, but I've no clue what she's trying to signal. Exasperated when she sees I can't understand her, she moves close and murmurs into my ear.

"We'll take them by surprise before they get curious to see what's happened to their friend. As soon as we get an eye line on them, you shoot the one on the right."

Bemused, I whisper back, "How do you know it should be the one on the right?"

Her eyes roll, but she manages to keep the sarcasm controlled and out of her voice. "There are only two. If I know which one you're taking out, I can concentrate on the other."

Okay. Right. I feel really dumb right now, but I've never been trained in battle, so maybe she'll give me a pass.

I understand the countdown when she holds three fingers

up and moves one down. As the third descends, we advance, side by side.

There are two men playing cards. Neither notices our entry. That doesn't stop Helo. She's got her arm wrapped around the throat of the man on the left, and just like his companion, slits his throat without pausing to take a breath.

Me? I freeze. Firing at a target is nothing like shooting at a person, knowing I'm going to take his life, or at the least, probably making him regret having to live the rest of it. How can I just kill a man who's been taken by surprise and who is currently sitting, jaw dropped, staring at his friend, who Helo just took out right in front of his eyes?

He's no threat, is he? It looks like he's just going to put his cards down and surrender...

The cards fall, and he indeed does raise his hands, but one has a gun in it. He shoots, but Helo's a moment too fast, or a moment too slow, depending on how you look at it. He doesn't make the chest shot he was aiming for, but the bullet catches her as she throws herself to one side.

I don't hesitate. The gunshot freed something inside me. In a split second, I've taken the stance Buzz drilled into my mind and fire three quick shots in succession. One in his head, two in his chest.

Then, I scream as twin thoughts slam into my mind. *I've killed a man, and Helo's been shot.*

"Helo!" I throw myself across the room to where she's landed flat on the ground. There's so much blood coming out of her. I'm not sure from where. I think she's breathing, but, oh, hell. "Helo, I'm so damn sorry."

She breathes in a breath, lets it out, and relief floods through me when I see her chest move. She opens her mouth. "Good shooting there, hon."

What?

"I'm sorry, so sorry," I start babbling, my hands reaching out to search where all the blood is coming from, but she puts out her hands to stop me.

"Jasmine," she says sharply. "Most of the blood is his." She points to the man who's throat she had cut. "The bullet only scratched my side. I'll live."

"You shouldn't have been shot at all. If I'd done what you asked..."

Reaching up, she cups her bloody hands around my cheeks. "Jasmine, breathe, honey. I'm just pleased that you shot him before he could finish the job. This is my world, not yours."

"It was your fuckin' world. It's not anymore."

Helo rolls, placing me under her at the unknown voice, an instinctive reaction I'm sure while smoothly taking the gun I'm holding from my hand into hers.

I stop breathing. *So close, yet so far.*

And then Helo starts laughing. "You wanna bet, man of mine? This is more fun than I'd had in years."

"I'll take that bet, my queen. 'Cause this is the last time I'm letting you out of my sight. And, damn it. You're bleeding, woman."

She's gently pulled off me by the man I belatedly recognise as Chaz, her old man and prez of the Arizona Soulz. And there, behind him, is another I recognise. I gulp when I see him.

My heart leaps, but I immediately ground myself. *Strider's not my future. He's my past.* I try to drown the embryonic hope that what Helo told me was true and that he really does want me.

It's hard to read the expression on his face, especially when his first words to me are spoken gruffly. "You hurt?"

I realise I, too, am covered with blood. "No. Helo's the only one who got injured." I don't add it's thanks to her I'm alive. That's a debt I'll probably be repaying all my life.

At my proclamation, he reaches down his hand, grabs mine, and pulls me to my feet.

But before he has a chance to say anything, Helo interrupts. "Boys," she starts casually, raising her chin first to Chaz, then to Strider. "We left one alive in the basement. Barclay Aster is dead, but one of his henchmen is there. Might have a fractured skull, but I'm sure you could get something from him." She winces, puts her hand to her injured side, then somehow summons up a grin for me. "Jasmine may be entitled to any legacy her ex-husband might have left."

"I want nothing from him," I spit out. His world's not mine. "I don't want any part of a criminal enterprise."

But Chaz and Strider share a glance with each other, and then Strider grins. "Your place or mine?"

Chaz chuckles. "Yours is nearer, but Helo needs sorting out."

"Got that handled." Shotgun comes back into sight. "Just called Rufus. He's got a medic on speed dial. I suggest you take Helo, get her looked at, while we take the package back to Austin. Rufus can also let us borrow a truck. We'll just get a prospect to return it to him." He pauses and grins at the blood splattered around. "After he's cleaned it properly, of course."

"We're just racking up favours to repay to Rufus," Chaz complains, but it's half-heartedly. Then, he cheers up. "But that's your problem, Strider."

The man he's addressing only seems to be half paying attention to the conversation. Instead, he's staring at me. He waves his hand which Chaz seems to take as agreement, then steps closer. Now I'm getting one hundred percent of his focus.

"I'm not married now." His voice is deadly serious.

It wasn't what I expected to come out of his mouth, but sympathy rushes through me. "I'm so sorry to hear about Anna. Helo told me." I can feel myself blush at the way the words tumble out. I hope they convey I'm genuinely sorry for him.

He shrugs. "I lost Anna years ago. I've been told it was guilt that made me stay with her. Maybe they're right. There's a hole in my heart, but it wasn't there when she finally left me. It appeared the day you walked away."

I'm dumbstruck. "You took me to see her to show me there was no room in your life for anyone else."

"I took you to see her so you'd understand I had nothing to offer. Hell, Jasmine. I hated myself after I made you abort our baby. I panicked. At the time, it felt right. But after? It didn't just tear you apart. It tore me into pieces. And, what was worse was knowing I'd made you do that as compensation to a woman who, even at that time, was beyond the point she'd ever understand. You could have had the baby, paraded it in front of her, and she wouldn't have given a damn."

"Helo said you thought you'd caused her condition." I offer it as support, not accusation.

Again, his shoulders rise and fall. "I couldn't see any other reason for it. If you're interested, Chaz has thought I've been an idiot all along. Punishing myself for something that probably wasn't even down to me. Even if the crash caused her illness, I hadn't lost control of the bike on purpose."

There's the rusty taste of blood in the air that I breathe and dead bodies around me. It seems an incongruous place to have such a talk now. But somehow, for us, it's right to have this conversation in a place of darkness. Maybe it's the start of us both finding our way back into the light.

And the right time for my confession. "I told myself I was leaving as you'd shown me how much you loved your wife and that there was no way I'd ever be able to measure up to her memory, even after she'd died." Strider goes to speak, but I let my words come out fast. "But I felt guilty too. I knew I was still married. I wasn't free. If I'd hung around until Anna died, even if you wanted me, you couldn't have me."

He surprises me when he spits out with vehemence, "It's a shame Barclay Aster is dead." As my mouth drops open, he continues, "I'd have wanted him alive, to tear him limb from limb myself. I'd have made him suffer tenfold for everything he put you through." His hands do that familiar action of pulling his hair back into a ponytail before letting it drop. "Why the fuck didn't you tell us about him and what he'd put you through?"

"He is, *was*," I make the correction with no little satisfaction, "a powerful man with powerful connections. The Wretched Soulz gave me sanctuary. How could I thank you by bringing the Mafia down on your head?" I look around and see Helo being helped out by Chaz, presumably being taken to see the medic they'd been talking about. "It seems like I now owe you my life. Somehow, you got Helo into the signing, so she was there when I needed help." I bite my lip, hoping she'll have no long-lasting repercussions.

He reads me so well as he tries to put my mind at ease. "Helo will be fine. But yeah..." he pauses to pull his hair back again. When it flops forward, he continues, "That book, when we realised it probably wasn't fiction, when Mayhem..." At my look of confusion, he explains, "The best data analyst around and a Soul from LA, well, when he discovered that you'd written a sanitised version of the truth, we had an inkling who we were dealing with. I wanted to talk to you and explain about Anna, but until you started making arrangements with StoryTeller's ol' lady, I had no idea how to find you. I was over the moon to know I had a chance to see you in Dallas—I'd planned to meet up with you after the signing." He pauses and his brow draws down. "Then we fuckin' realised if we knew where you'd be, so would anyone else who was looking for you.

So..." he breaks off, his face lightens and he grins. "Chaz offered his secret weapon. His woman."

"I'll never be able to repay what I owe you."

He moves closer. "I know ways you can try. Be my woman, Jasmine. Agree to be my ol' lady, and now we're both free, my wife."

CHAPTER SEVENTEEN
STRIDER

I hold my breath, waiting for Jasmine to answer, but we're interrupted by a commotion as the man who Helo disabled downstairs is brought up, trussed like a Thanksgiving turkey, but struggling despite his bindings. They haven't thought to gag him, so he's swearing up a storm.

It's a stark reminder of where we are and who I am.

While Jasmine already knows more about the Soulz than Anna ever did, I have an overwhelming need to shield her from the dark side of MC life. Worried that she'd never agree to stay with me if she sees what I truly can be like.

Wanting to hide her from any further distress, I move close, pulling her to me, turning her face into my chest to protect her from the sight of him being manhandled. But I can't block out her ears, and I shout, "Shut him up."

Jasmine struggles in my hold. I don't want to hurt her, so I allow her to get loose. She pulls away from me and spits on the man who Shotgun and Buzz have firmly in their hold. Turning to me, she states, "I want to be there when you question him. I want to hear about everything Barclay planned. Everything he was involved in."

"No," I refute softly. "Jas, you really don't want to see or hear that."

She regards me haughtily. "No? Strider, I've just heard he's left me a legacy, and I'm entitled to know what. And don't you think for a moment that I can't imagine the types of persuasion you'll use. I might even have some ideas of my own. A man says a lot when he's threatened with the loss of his balls or dick."

It's not only me unable to hide a hiss, but her words have me rearranging my thoughts.

Anna never wanted to be involved in the club. She'd never set foot in the clubhouse, let alone when we had our parties. But Jasmine's already been exposed to all that. My inner man wants to protect her like I had my deceased wife, but now I realise, Jasmine's cut from a different cloth. She's not lived a protected life. She's been exposed to horrors I don't want to think about.

She's proving herself stronger than I ever expected. She's proving herself as...

Shotgun puts it into words. "That, there, Prez, is an ol' lady worth the title."

I raise my eyes to the heavens, then look down at her. Hoping to fuck I'm reading her right and not making yet another misstep, I lean down and speak directly into her ear so only she can hear me. I offer, "I accept. Full involvement. But only if you let me fuck you first."

She draws in air as she gasps. Her cheeks flush. She looks down, then raises her gaze to me. "Your wife only died a short while ago. My husband less than an hour ago. My head's in no space to make decisions right now. I can't agree to be your old lady, let alone your wife. But if your other offer is still on the table, then after months of being alone and only able to use my vibrator, then I think working out our sexual frustrations sounds nice."

Nice? If I can only get such an insignificant rating, I need to up my game. *Nice* wasn't the way I'd describe our previous encounters. Instead of being annoyed or abashed, my cock starts to thicken as I think of ways I can improve her assessment. But I'm sure not going to awe her with my prowess in an unknown clubhouse or anonymous hotel room. I need to get her back to Austin.

Shotgun and Buzz have just disappeared with the man they brought up from the basement as Rufus's prospect had delivered the promised truck, then disappeared just as we'd requested.

"Let's go," I tell her, suddenly in a rush to get her back to my club, my room, my bed. I'm going to fuck her so good she'll never again want to leave me.

She chuckles at my impatience and, taking the hand that I offer, comes out into the sweet fresh air.

Outside, Shotgun and Buzz are waiting. Sounds from the truck show our prisoner is already in the back. When I stop and gesture that she should get into the passenger side, she balks.

"You really want me to ride with him?" she asks scornfully.

Chastised, I admit, "They're going back to Austin…"

"So are you," she interrupts. "I want to ride with you."

I haven't had a woman on the back of my bike since the day I'd crashed and Anna had come off. I'm certainly not going to risk Jasmine. "No," I reply. "No one rides with me."

When Jassy's hands go to her hips, I realise I've got a battle on my hands. "No?" Her first word sounds innocent. As I start to nod my head, she cuts off anything I might say. "You just asked me to be your old lady, but then say I can't ride with you?"

I think that's exactly what I just said. Gritting my teeth, I tell her, "It's too risky."

"Then you give up riding your bike."

Me? "Woman," I snarl. "I've been riding for years—"

"Exactly." She prods her finger into my chest as if making a point. "You had an accident when you were still new to bikes. I don't think there's any risk to me by riding with you after all the years' experience you've now had than behind any other man on a bike."

She'll never be fucking riding with anyone else.

Shotgun overhears. "You can ride with me, sweetheart. Buzz can drive the truck."

Oh no, she won't.

"Thanks, Shotgun," she calls back. "I'd appreciate that."

My hands clench into fists as a roar bursts out of me. "The only bike you'll be getting on is mine."

Jasmine's face splits into a wide grin. "Well, that's settled then."

Fuck me. I'm totally fucked with this woman. I know Anna used to use ploys to get what she wanted from me, but the difference with Jasmine is she's only prodding me in the direction I really want to go. I want her on my bike. I want to feel her arms wrapped around my waist. I'm just terrified of history repeating itself.

Grabbing her hand, I lead her over to my bike. Taking my helmet off the handlebars, I hand it to her.

"Uh-huh," she tells me, handing it back. "Don't want you breaking your head."

"Fuckin' wear it, woman." I slam it down on her skull and buckle it before she can protest again.

It's only a half-head, and while it does fine for me, it's in no way sufficient for her. Once I set off, instead of heading straight home, I stop at the first motorcycle dealer I come to. Taking her inside, I check out the helmets on display and pick out one complete with a visor. Her look of derision makes me grin.

In the end, we do settle for a full face, but one where the whole front lifts up so she doesn't feel claustrophobic. I then buy her a full set of leathers so she can avoid road rash if she happens to come off. I can see her laughing at me, but along with her mirth, there's understanding and compassion. She lets me have my way, going over the top with her protection.

I've blamed myself for years for Anna's condition. Maybe I'm right. Maybe I'm wrong. But I'm taking no chances with Jasmine.

Having made our detour, my brothers are already way ahead of us on the road to Austin. Unusually, for once, I'm unescorted on the road, which means there's no one to see me riding embarrassingly like an old woman. I do no more than fifty, even on the freeway. It should take me under four hours to make the journey. I end up taking five. When I stop three-quarters of the way home to top off my tank, Jasmine looks at me and laughs.

"I think I could walk faster."

"Woman! I'm trying to keep you safe." I go inside to pay. When I come out, she leans close to me.

"And I'm just impatient to get fucked."

Rolling my eyes, I start the engine. I do increase the speed a little as she's raised an urgency inside me. But there's a bone-deep worry deep inside me that lightning, perhaps, can indeed strike twice.

When we finally reach the clubhouse, I breathe a sigh of relief. Without me having to tell her, she gets off the bike before I paddle walk it back into my space. I notice her hands going to the small of her back as she stretches and realise it was quite a long journey for someone unaccustomed to riding. But no complaint comes out of her mouth.

Instead, she pushes up the front of her helmet, winks, holds out her hand, and when I take it, she starts to drag me inside.

Oh hell, yeah, baby. My cock is already at full mast.

We enter the club room which is crowded.

"Nice lid!" Shotgun calls out. He grabs at his belly and doubles over laughing.

Unsure of herself now, Jasmine fumbles at the buckle, and I help her to get the helmet off.

"I told you it was too much," she hisses, trying to hide the offending article behind her back.

Seeing the damage he's done, Shotgun crosses the room to us. "If I'm ever lucky enough to find a woman half your worth, Jassy, she'll be wearing one just like that. Prez knows he's got precious cargo."

Strangely, even I can see he's sincere. Maybe my accident with Anna was a warning to us all. Not that women's heads are more fragile than ours, but we're just stupid asses who take risks with our lives. Wearing just skull caps, or nothing at all, as we don't need to in Texas. Our ladies? Well, their lives are worth more than ours.

Uncomfortable with the scrutiny she's attracting, Jasmine stands on tiptoe to speak into my ear. "I'm cooking in these leathers. I need to take them off."

A lewd grin that I can't prevent spreads over my face. "Being naked will help," I murmur back.

Her face flushes and it's not just heat from the clothing. Not wanting to waste any more time, it's me taking her hand now, dragging her through the brothers who part to make us a path. Chuckles and laughter follow us, not one person in any doubt as to our intentions.

It's only when I reach my room that I realise I'm nervous. I've had Jasmine here many times before. She was the club girl who caught my attention, then, without me realising it, she became so much more. Sex isn't just what I want from her. I always wanted it all. But with Anna still breathing, I had nothing to offer.

She's rightly holding back from making a commitment. I've got to show her she's my everything and nowhere close to being second best.

I know why she wants to fuck. I've served. I've seen death, suffering, and have had my lucky escapes at the wrong end of the gun or just being a foot away from a landmine. It makes you want to celebrate life in the most basic of ways. Barclay could have killed her today. If Helo hadn't been with her, he could have given her to his men to sexually torture and fuck knows what else. The blood thrums through my veins, wanting to claim her, wanting to mark her as mine, wanting no man to ever touch her again.

But she needs this in the same way as a man who's seen war. She wants sex, her body's release to remind her she's survived.

The only times she's been in this room, the dynamic has been as a club girl and the prez. I stuck to those boundaries. My emotions only evident because after we'd had our pleasure, I hadn't kicked her out of my bed. Many times, I'd woken up snuggling her, but I still kept my distance.

Now? Now I see her. She's no substitute for my wife. If Anna hadn't become ill, if I'm honest, she wouldn't have still been part of my life. The club's too important to me. Jasmine would never ask me to give it up. She embraces it. Loves it.

And, even though she doesn't appreciate how much, she's earned the affection and respect of my men.

Something shifts inside me as I see her doing something she's done a hundred times before. Taking off her clothes and getting naked, just like a club girl. My heart twists, and I move toward her. "Let me."

She's already taken off her leather jacket. Now I help her to remove her new chaps. Then I pause, just staring at her. She seems awkward and looks away from my scrutiny. Placing my hand on her cheek, I turn her back to face me.

"Have I ever told you how fuckin' beautiful you are?" I haven't. That would have been a step too far. "I should have done so, Jasmine. But it's not just your beauty that I fell for. It's the whole package."

She flinches for some reason. "There's no need for fancy words, Strider. I'm a sure bet."

But I want to give her everything. Her being in danger, me coming too fucking close to losing her forever, had knocked sense into my head. Anna had been my teenage sweetheart. Jasmine is my adult relationship.

As if I'm taking too long, she takes hold of the bottom of her t-shirt and starts to move it up over her head. I put my hands on hers. "Let me love you," I implore. "Let me worship you."

I've fucked things up. I might never have said words that expressed my feelings, but I'd always made love to Jasmine. It had never been just sex. Her words in her book had described how the club girl fell for the prez, and how her feelings were reciprocated. Only, in real life, instead of talking to her, I'd made the misstep of taking her to see Anna. In real life, I'd been stupid. If I was as good as the fictional prez, I'd have talked to her, admitted my emotions, and explained why I couldn't, then, make her mine.

I've got her rattled now. She's not sure whether I want her naked or not. There was never any hesitation between us. There was only going to be one result when I called a club girl to my bed.

While her wide eyes stare at me, I gradually ease up her t-shirt. When I reveal her bra, instead of ripping it off, I lower my head and mouth her nipples through the lacy material. She reacts now, murmuring in pleasure.

Taking my time as if this was a woman I needed to impress, one I've never had in my bed before, I worship her breasts, her neck, her shoulders with kisses and caresses that leave her moaning for more. She's still holding herself stiffly as though trying to disassociate from my tenderness. I'm determined to wear her down. Using her hair to tilt her head to one side, I nibble at the side of her throat.

A moan escapes and my road name on a sigh. "Strider."

"Call me Colt," I murmur into her neck. "I'm not the prez of the club when you're with me. I'm just a man who adores you."

"Strider,' she repeats again, emphasising the two syllables.

I'm certain that in a short while, I'm going to hear the name that I want coming out of her mouth.

CHAPTER EIGHTEEN
JASMINE

Strider's been saying things that I've so often dreamed about hearing. After the last few months, when I tried to get him out of my mind by reminding myself he was committed to somebody else and always would be in this world and the next, I couldn't let down my guard and let myself believe him.

When I left him, I hurt so damn badly I thought my heart would never mend. The only men I'd had any time for were the ones who existed in my head and who I painted onto the canvas of my novels. He's spoiled me for anyone else, but I'd hoped in time I would forget him, and be able to move on.

If it hadn't been for Barclay and today's violence, I wouldn't have weakened and let myself come back with him. For a moment, I must have lost my damn senses when I pushed him to let me ride on his bike. If I hadn't known the story of the accident he'd previously had, I'd have been surprised at how carefully he was riding. Even though we hadn't gone fast, I'd loved every minute. I'd felt I was dreaming, flying down the road with my hands wrapped around his waist.

Everything he's done, everything he's said since the moment he came back into my life, has been exactly what I've always hoped to hear. But it would destroy me if I was being optimistic for no reason.

I thought if I could reduce this to a simple fuck, it would give him a way out without the organ that keeps my blood flowing around my body being shattered for good.

He said he wants me to be his old lady and his wife. Oh, how I wish I could believe him. For some reason I can't, even though he's said all the right things, and by God, the way he's touching me now, caressing me with his touches and cajoling me with his words. I want to trust him, but I must stay detached to protect myself.

But oh, it's so hard.

When he asks me to call him his government name, I refuse. It's an intimate step too far.

Then, as his hands finally, but slowly, unclasp my bra, he weighs my breasts in his palms, for a moment just staring at them as though he'd never seen them before. "You're so fuckin' beautiful," he rasps before reapplying his attention to the nipples he already knows are sensitive as hell. The way he's pinching, sucking, and licking makes me wonder if I could orgasm from just his touch there.

Wetness rushes through me, and my clit throbs. I try to rub my thighs together in order to ease the ache. He chuckles, *the bastard.* He knows exactly how he's winding me up.

Straightening, he moves his lips away from my breasts and settles them on my mouth. His tongue demands entry, and I can't resist. I've so missed his taste. There's no other word to describe what he's doing other than to say he's devouring me. I can't pull away. I'm no unwilling participant and I give it my all. Tongues duel, teeth clash, and I know my lips will be bruised in the morning. My nostrils are full of a perfume that's uniquely his, and my body responds as though my brain has nothing to do with it. There's a rumbling coming from his chest, and when he starts to pull back, I grasp him to me, unable to get enough of him.

He chuckles and then gives me what I want, coming in to kiss me some more.

Of its own volition, my left leg rises off the floor and bends to wrap around his lower limbs, pulling him closer, then shamelessly, I'm trying to rub myself against him.

Again, his mouth leaves mine, but only enough to whisper gruffly, "If we keep on like this, then I'm going to come in my pants like a teenage boy."

At least I'm not alone in my suffering. "Guess we both better get naked then," I suggest.

"Always knew you were smart," he replies, the mirth discernible in his voice. "I, er, kind of need to let you go for that."

Taking his point, I reluctantly return my foot to the floor and ease away from him. But when I go to unzip my jeans, his hands are already there. And when he's got them undone, he lowers both my pants, panties, and himself to the floor, leaning forward so his face is right in my crotch, and then he inhales.

"Fuckin' best scent in the world," he states, as if to himself.

My jeans are around my ankles, making it difficult for me to move, and his proximity to my nether regions is no help at all to my state of arousal. He seems to be enjoying himself, breathing me in once more.

"Strider," I whine. He's not the only one wanting to relearn what we'd enjoyed so many times before. I want to see if his cock is just as good as I remember.

He pauses, then huffs a breath making my clit twitch. I'm so fucking close and he's barely touched me at all. "What did I tell you to call me?"

"Strider, please. Can we just fuck?"

He chuckles, the vibration all but setting me off. "Not going to fuck you. We're going to make love."

"I don't care what you call it," I cry out. "Just take me now."

"Ask me."

"Strider…"

He makes a grunt of disapproval and touches me *right there.*

Oh, Jesus, help me, but I can't prevent his name escaping my mouth in a half-scream. "Colt."

He lifts me, carries me to the bed and lies me gently down. He removes my boots then my jeans. At last, he pulls my panties off my ankles.

All action stops. I've been writhing in anticipation, head thrown back, eyes closed. After a moment, I lift up to glare at him. He's staring at me with such reverence it takes my breath away. If the author part of me was trying to describe a look of adoration, then that's what I'm seeing here. His lips are curved in pleasure, his eyes hooded, his cheeks flushed. His jaw tightens as he gives a little shake of his head.

"It should be criminal to have such a glorious pussy."

I snort. "Hey, fella. Perhaps you can touch it and worship it rather than just stare at it."

He catches my eye. "Say, please, Colt."

I've already capitulated and don't want to delay anymore. "Please, Colt."

I rest my head back down, but still, he holds back.

"You want me to eat your pussy?"

I'm half-annoyed, half-amused and taut with expectation. "Please, Colt," I repeat.

I must have forgotten how talented this man is with his tongue, as within moments, my muscles are spasming. My reaction spurs him on. He licks my clit and puts a finger inside me, and then one more. He knows exactly where to curl around to hit that spot that drives me wild.

I scream and bend forward, the orgasm so extreme it's almost too hard to bear. My vibrator hadn't compensated at all for the loss of him over the past months. As my body tenses and releases with aftershocks, he brings me back to earth.

"I've got to get inside you." His voice is gruff.

"I want you." I can't wait to feel that large cock of his again. My arousal is building up at the thought of welcoming it back like an old friend. Strider, *Colt*, has moves, and I want him to remind me of them.

I hear boots falling to the floor, a zipper being lowered, then the rustle of fabric. Watching him through lazy eyes, I see his tee ripped over his head.

He hasn't changed at all since I last saw him naked, though maybe he's even more delicious than he was before. He's a big man, but it's all hard-earned muscle.

Bringing his body down over me, I feel his dick against my entrance.

I bat my hands against him and shout, "Condom!"

He rears back. "You're not on the pill?"

"Not since I left here. It didn't seem worth it." And just to make sure I've made it clear, I say, "There's been nobody else."

He looks like he's battling with himself. His mouth works, then he swallows as if changing his mind about what words to use. He's still as a statue when he raises his eyes, closes them, then opens them again as he looks down. Seriousness is written all over his features.

"There's nothing more I'd like than a child with you." He places his finger over my lips. "I know with all the past that comes between us that you're unsure. I'll protect you for now," his lips quirk, "as best as I'm able to." It makes me remember that it was a condom that broke before. "I'll wait until you're certain of me, Jasmine. But please, understand, a future with you, a family, is what I want."

He doesn't wait for my response, which is lucky, as I've no idea what to say. Raising his body off mine, he leaves the bed and rummages in a drawer. "Must be some in here somewhere." Finally, he fishes some out. He squints and holds them up to the light. "They're still in date, thank fuck."

Wait a moment. Sitting up, I narrow my eyes. "When was the last time you used them?"

Looking at me, he shrugs. "Last time you were in my bed, Jassy. Ain't been anyone else."

Wow. As I watch him roll on the latex, I realise I'd been sure that while I was pretty certain he hadn't had anyone else while I was still in the club—club girls aren't known for being discreet—I'd convinced myself he'd have had a revolving door on his bedroom once he'd known I was gone for sure.

His task finished, he looks up and meets my eyes. "Didn't want anyone else, Jasmine. And I knew it was only a matter of time before I found you again. Wasn't going to stop looking."

As he repositions himself and eases inside me, I close my eyes, relishing the feeling that's like coming home. When he starts to move inside me, my body responds automatically, meeting thrust for thrust. It's slow, as he promised. It's not a frenzied coupling. It's making love.

He's worshiping me with his slow penetration, making me feel loved.

So different from our first time together. I was a club girl, there not even for a night, just for the time it took for him to get off. I knew the score and wasn't disappointed. Next night, it was the same, the following no different. I don't know when it happened, but slowly, it changed, so gradually, I didn't really notice. He was always a generous lover, not expecting a club girl to be disappointed. But he didn't need to go down on me, didn't need to kiss me, didn't need to make me feel like I was cherished.

And that's exactly what he's making me feel now. Cherished.

CHAPTER NINETEEN
STRIDER

Mid-thrust, I pause. "You are cherished. You always were."

She gasps. "I didn't mean to say that out loud."

I chuckle and resume the slow pushing in and pulling out. It's keeping both our arousal amped up without letting us go over. I want this to last, even though I'm on a hair trigger. I know my pace is ramping up the desire inside her, and when she lets go, I'll be experiencing something out of this world.

"I took a club girl into my bed," I tell her, in a soothing tone. "Soon knew I wanted no one else to have her. See, she had this magical pussy that put all other women out of my mind. No one who'd come before her could compare." I hope she understands what I'm saying. I mean, not even Anna, my wife. "I was fuckin' addicted. I wanted to make sure the club girl wasn't tempted to go elsewhere by using my best moves on her."

As I pause, she snorts. "It worked. It ruined me for all others."

I'm still slowly moving inside her, testing my controls in ways I never have. But maybe this is the moment when I can persuade her. So I take a risk. "Anna was my childhood sweetheart. Neither of us had much experience when we got together. Sex, we thought, was okay. But now I know I wasn't giving her everything I had to offer, and she was holding something back. We outgrew each other. If..."

"If it hadn't been for the accident, her decline, and your guilt that you'd caused her condition." I pause my movement as she continues, "You told Chaz. Chaz told Helo, and Helo tried to make sense of it."

"Yeah." Resuming my unhurried pace, I press in again. "I fucked up, made another misstep when I took you to see her. Well, not that, but that I didn't explain myself. I couldn't... I couldn't find the words to tell you that I loved you more than her, but it wasn't the time to explain."

Her vagina compresses around me, making me gasp. "I didn't want to be second best."

I thrust in harder. "Never second best. There's been no one like you. No one who's accepted me for who I am, and who loves my club. No one who I want to talk to, let alone make love. I fuckin' want you in my life, Jasmine."

She clenches again. "For fuck's sake, can we stop talking?"

I grab my chance. Rolling my hips, pushing in deep, and holding still for a moment, I say, "Tell me you're mine."

She screams, "I'm fucking yours!"

That releases something inside me. I let go, pounding into her, into *my* woman, into the old lady, wife, who's going to be beside me forever. I'm never letting her go. For a moment, I damn the condom, as I want my release to be inside her, marking her as mine.

The air is filled with grunts, moans and the combination of both our odours. She accepts everything I give her and pushes for more. She's tight, responsive, and I hold on until I feel her go taut, muscles gripping, rippling around my dick. I let out a roar as cum shoots from my balls and into her cunt.

I've spent many nights with Jasmine, but none topped this. I see stars, hell, the whole fucking universe, and it's a good few seconds before I come back to myself.

"Jesus." I rest my forehead down on hers.

"Mmm mmm." Her satisfied murmur settles my worries that it was just as good for her.

We stay like that until I feel my dick softening. "Got to go take care of business," I warn her.

"Hmm."

I kinda like I've robbed her of coherent speech. I hold the end of the condom, pull out, then, "Oh fuckin' hell."

"Mmm. What?"

There's no easy way to tell her. "Condom broke."

Her body goes rigid. Putting my arms around her, I pull her up and hold her tight. "Whatever happens, I'm there with you. I meant what I said. Whatever the outcome is, I want it."

She starts shaking. I worry she's going into shock until I realise what the sounds are that she's making. She's laughing.

"Guess we've just got to accept Fate's got a hand in this."

Relieved, I kiss her hair, holding her close. I admit my most secret thoughts. "I really, really like fucking you bare."

When she doesn't immediately answer, I decide I'll need to get new condoms. Find the best-rated brand, or, heaven forbid, have to wait until she goes back on the pill.

She cups her hands around my cheeks, looks into my eyes, and says, "Guess I better agree to be your old lady if it turns out we're going to have a kid."

Resisting the urge to fist pump the air, I press my advantage. "And my wife."

She punches my arm. "Better up your game, Colt, if that's your idea of a proposal."

Chuckling, I respond, "Don't worry, I've got ideas on exactly how to do it right. Just wanted to make sure I wasn't going to be embarrassed if you turned me down."

She turns and looks at me sleepily. "With a cock like yours, I'd be an idiot."

"You like my cock?"

"Fucking love your cock."

Said item has roused itself back to life again. With a raised eyebrow, I query her. Her answering expression shows her thoughts match mine. Not much point using potentially defective condoms. I fuck her bare, and hell, if I already thought she was the best, I've now reason to rethink again.

After another points-winning session, we fall asleep, arms around each other. I never slept as well as when she's in my bed, and tonight's no different. When I wake in the small hours, I can't help pushing my ready cock against her soft ass. The action wakes her, and we pleasure each other again. I can't think of anything better than coming inside her. No other woman, including my wife, has made me feel so good, so satisfied.

Thank fuck I found her, and before Barclay was able to take her completely out of my life. I just wish I'd been there and able to make him suffer.

My Jasmine's a survivor.

Morning comes, and I've lain awake for a while beside her with one question on my mind.

When she finally wakes, stretches, and looks at me with that beautiful smile, I ask, "What do you want me to call you?" When her eyebrows rise, I explain, "I've always known you as Jasmine, yet your real name is Katrina. Do you want to revert to that?"

She lengthens her arms over her head, then pulls them back down to her sides. Her brow furrows, and she doesn't immediately answer.

"No pressure. You don't have to decide now."

"I'll need to be Katrina," she muses, "to get my father's legacy. Not that I want it, but maybe there's some good I can do with it. But Katrina is in my past. I rather like the Jasmine I am now. It's the life I chose for myself."

For some reason, that pleases me. "I love Jasmine. I love you, Jasmine. Kind of don't like thinking of you as anyone else."

"I remade myself when I left Barclay," she says firmly. "And I don't ever want to go back."

"You'll never have to. I meant it when I said you were mine. You've got a family now."

"Wretched Soulz?"

Chuckling softly, I reply, "The brothers knew you were mine even before I did."

Biting her lip, she tells me, "I'm sorry I ran."

"I'm fuckin' sorry I only read half the book. If I'd gotten to the end, I'd never have let you go."

"Oh, Colt." I notice my real name comes to her lips more easily now. "I shouldn't have told my own story."

"If you hadn't, where would you be now?" I contradict. "If you hadn't given us the clues, we'd never have come looking for you."

I hate the full-body shudder she gives. I hate the look in her eyes that shows she's imagining how differently things could have turned out. So, I take her mind off it. Placing her hand on my cock, I show her what I want. When I slide my arms under her body, positioning her on her hands and knees, she doesn't object. When I slide inside her, she gasps.

"More, Colt. More."

Last night was amazing. This morning tops that. Christ, I don't know how I'll survive the intensity of my orgasms with her. It's as if now I've admitted my feelings for her, I can't hold anything back.

Again I see stars and I don't regret it.

We doze for a while, then are disturbed by a knock on my door.

"Prez? Chaz has arrived," a prospect calls

There's only one reason he's here. That's to question the man who's currently held in our basement.

"I've gotta go, sweetheart." It's only club business that will ever drag me out of our bed.

"Go do your stuff," she tells me, planting a kiss on my lips, then rolls over. "I'll catch up on my sleep. You wore me out."

Gazing at her for a moment, feeling the pride only a man can at satisfying his woman, I leave the bed, dress, and take the trek to the clubhouse. There, I greet Chaz with back slaps and a polite handshake to his woman.

"You okay, Helo?"

She hangs onto her man's arm, whose face has twisted into a snarl. "I'm fine. Just a few stitches. How's Jasmine?"

"Sleeping," I tell her.

"Good." She nods. "I suppose there's somewhere I can get coffee?"

I yell for a prospect and make sure they know to keep our guest happy

"Fuckin' women," Chaz confides. "Helo should be resting, but there's no arguing with her. She wanted to come to see Jasmine and make sure she's alright." As I pause to open the door to where our captive is held, he puts his hand on my arm. "You pulled your head out of you ass?"

Another man I might have hit for his question, but it's

Chaz, who I've known for a very long time. "Sure have," I tell him. "Jasmine's going to be mine."

He gives a sharp nod. "Then let's make sure all loose ends are tied up."

Raising my chin, I gesture Chaz should go in front of me and guide him out through the clubhouse, along a concrete path, then enter our gym. He stops inside, looking confused. Chuckling, I point the way to where an exercise mat has been raised off the floor. Rapping on the trapdoor, it opens, and I nod that Chaz should descend the stairs.

At the bottom, he looks around with admiration. "Nice setup you've got here." He'd appreciate it, but other people, particularly our *guests,* not so much. The walls are bare, painted in a special paint that's easy to wash down. The floor, currently covered in plastic, tilts toward a drain in the center. Looking up, it's easy to see the insulation that keeps any sound from getting out. When he finishes his inspection, he asks, "Cops ever find it?"

"Nah," I reply. "It's survived a few searches of the club when feds have gotten overly nosy."

"Reminds me of the Satan's Devils." He chuckles. "They've got their armoury under what looks like a filled-in swimming pool. Never been discovered."

"Drummer's lot?" When he raises his chin, I note quite seriously, "I think I'd like to have a good conversation with that man someday."

"He's sound," Chaz agrees. He turns his attention to our current guest who's hanging from some handy hooks we'd driven into the ceiling.

I, too, am all business now. "Take off his gag," I instruct. Tequila leaps to do my bidding.

The man looks around, then fixes his eyes on me and Chaz. "You've got to let me down. I've got a concussion."

"Yeah? Well, my woman gave you that." Chaz sounds happy and totally unrepentant.

Ignoring the Arizona prez, the man starts looking around for anyone who might be more sympathetic. "You have no idea who you're dealing with. My boss won't like having one of his men fucked with."

I realise he's got no idea he's the last man standing, the only one of Aster's crew who kidnapped Jasmine and Helo to still be alive. And, no inclination his boss, as powerful as he thinks he might be, is already dead.

"Your boss is in no position to object." I shrug my shoulders as I tell him. "Which reminds me, Buzz. Where is Aster now?"

Buzz grins widely. "Dallas mortuary. Poor fucker had a car accident and somehow ended up with a broken neck."

The man's mouth gapes open. "You're lying." His voice has less strength in it than previously.

Stepping forward, I take the initiative. "What's your name?" I snap.

His backbone puts in an appearance. "What's it to you?"

"Nothing." Again, my shoulders nonchalantly rise and lower. "Just thought you might like it written on your grave-stone." He pales. I decide to end all speculation now. "You're a dead man. You're not getting out of here. The only choice you've got is how hard you make it for yourself. You can go quick and easy, or we can keep you alive for weeks." Pausing, I turn to face Tequila. "What's our record?"

My enforcer seems to think for a moment before nodding his head. "Three weeks, two days. Hell, there was no bone left unbroken and barely any blood in his body."

"We burned him alive in the end," Buzz throws at him as if he needed to be reminded.

The man looks from one to the other of us, then at all the

other members standing around. There's no indication that we're yanking his chain or joking. That's because we're not. It's only moments before he yells, "I'm Clyde," as if deciding he should cooperate. We've certainly gotten to him if the stream of urine darkening his pants is any indication.

Chaz jerks his head to the side. Taking the hint, I step to the back of the room, inclining my ear so he can talk into it. I listen for a moment in total agreement, then step back and again take centre stage.

"Now, Clyde, I'm forgetting my manners. You've introduced yourself, but I haven't reciprocated. My name's Strider, and just in case you can't read our cuts, I'm the president of the Wretched Soulz Texas Charter. And this," I indicate Chaz, "is the prez of the Arizona Soulz. Perhaps you've been so buried in the mob that you haven't kept up with anything else. The Soulz have charters all over the United States and internationally." He's paled. Of course he knows, but it doesn't hurt to give him a reminder. "I think you'll find your mob you're so proud of would pale into insignificance beside our combined strength."

Clyde swallows hard, making his Adam's apple bob. His headache seems forgotten. I wonder how hard he's going to play it. He must realise no one's coming to rescue him, and if he'd been listening to Chaz and my discussion earlier, even if his cohorts made it onto the compound, they'd never find our torture chamber.

"Tell us everything you know. All the names, all the businesses."

"I can't!" His voice is a little above a whisper.

I need to hurry this along. I've got far better things I could be doing, like a woman I can't wait to get back inside. "He's all yours, Teq."

With no expression on his face, Tequila steps forward. As

fast as lightning, he grabs Clyde's hand and cuts off two fingers. As they drop to the ground, Clyde screams.

"We're not fuckin' around." My statement probably isn't necessary, as I think the enforcer has gotten his point across.

Tequila, his face still impassive, addresses him directly. "Just so you know, I'm good at my job. I know exactly how many parts I can cut off before you start to bleed out. And then, I'll be getting the blowtorch to cauterise your wounds to keep you alive."

It takes longer than I'd hoped. Clyde's lost the fingers and thumbs on both hands, and one arm now ends at a wrist, with the smell of burning flesh as Tequila had done just as he'd promised to stop the blood flow. Eventually, Clyde gets the point that even if he gets out of here alive, his life is probably not going to be worth living.

When he starts speaking, it's as if he can't stop. We've got the names of everyone Barclay Aster had been dealing with, a list of all the businesses he owned, all his connections, and the nice little titbit that Barclay was in debt to his Mafia bosses.

When he's been drained of all information, Tequila cuts his throat.

Buzz breaks the silence. "Well, that went well. I thought Prez would shoot him in the head."

He gets my middle finger pointed at him while I suppress a grin, considering he's probably got a point. Maybe, having Jasmine back in my life means I'm back in control.

CHAPTER TWENTY
JASMINE

"Mrs. Aster, I'm so sorry for your loss."

Unable to act like the grieving widow, I wave his condolences off. "We've been separated a while."

The lawyer nods as if it's of no consequence and turns to the well-dressed man sitting to my left-hand side. "And my sympathies to you too, Mr. D'Angelo."

"There's no need. We were business partners, not friends." Michael D'Angelo—his real name, I kid you not—glances toward me, his eyes narrowed in disgust. We've learned a lot about each other during the week since Barclay died. He's the consigliere of the local Mafia family, answerable only to the Don himself.

To my right sits Strider, looking totally out of place in his customary worn denim jeans, motorcycle boots, T-shirt and cut. While the Italian is dressed in a sharp dark grey suit, which I suspect is something like Armani, individually tailored, of course. A crisp white shirt, silk tie, and gold cufflinks complete the look.

Michael is an attractive man—sharp features, aquiline nose, hair expensively cut and styled. He's the same height as Strider but doesn't have his bulk. Though I suspect anyone would be wrong to underestimate his strength. He oozes confidence from every pore, and from the moment I first met him, I knew he was a man you'd think twice about arguing with. His words are measured, each one thought out before being delivered so they can't be misconstrued.

He's a male among males. Other men instinctively know this, straightening their backs when he walks into a room as if they don't want to come up lacking. Only Strider and Chaz seem unaffected, their self-assurance matching his.

The lawyer starts talking in some kind of legalise, and I let my mind drift. We all know what we're about to be told. The Mafia and the Soulz had written Barclay's will, hackers from both parties working together to forge both his and witnesses' signatures. After the negotiations were completed, though an original hadn't been thought to be in existence, Barclay's home and office had mysteriously burned to the ground. Something Michael hadn't been surprised about.

I think back to when I'd met him.

Strider hadn't wanted me anywhere near the Mafia man, but I'd reminded him I had a right to be included. I'd been riled I hadn't been able to question Barclay's guard, so this time, I wouldn't be missing out.

As I'd walked through the door, Michael's eyes had widened, and he'd stepped forward to take my hand, raising it to his lips.

"Bella." He lowers his head and lets his lips linger on the back of my hand. Behind me, Strider growls, but he still takes his time in straightening and maintains the touch of his fingers around mine. "Barclay was a damn fool. He had a tesoro, but by his own foolishness let it slip through his hands. If I'd seen you first—"

"She's mine," Strider interrupts.

Michael laughs and finally lets go of my hand. "And for that, I truly envy you." He points to a table. "Now let's all sit and get down to business."

I'm placed between Strider and Chaz, which puts me straight across from Michael. He knows full well what he's doing when he catches my eye and winks. I blush, and again, a rumble comes from my man.

Refreshments are brought in—coffee and delicious looking cannoli with a variety of fillings. My mouth waters at the chocolate-filled one, and I can't resist reaching out to take it.

The men content themselves with coffee and start to talk while I'm licking the delicious essence off my fingers. Again, I spot Michael staring straight at me. After shaking his head, he clears his throat and then turns his attention to Strider. "This could all be solved simply. Katrina could be placed under my protection." I read the undertone of his words, he probably means under him literally. I'm not blind to the very male interest I see in his eyes. While he's a good-looking man, he's certainly not the one for me.

"Katrina," I point at myself, "is not a commodity to be bought and sold."

At the same time, Strider says, "Already told you, Katrina belongs to me."

Chaz says nothing, just looks on, his face fixed and intent.

Chuckling, Michael takes a sip of his coffee. "Worth a shot," he begins, then sighs. "So how do we sort this mess out?" He brushes his hand back through his short hair, which remarkably stays in place. "Abraham James, Katrina's father, got into debt with Barclay Aster. Aster used some dubious methods to increase interest and keep raising the debt." He pauses, then frowns. "Unbeknownst to me." As Strider goes to speak, he raises his hand. "I'm not lily white. I admit my business practices range from grey to black, but we have a code, and when we give our word, we live by it. Aster manipulated James until he got what he wanted from him, his daughter." He points at me. "You."

Well, he couldn't have been talking about anyone else. Though the testosterone in the room is almost suffocating, I'm moved to speak. "Then he controlled me by continuing to increase my father's debt."

Michael nods as if I've been an attentive pupil. "Exactly. And your father took his own life so that you could get free, which meant Aster's cash cow had died. That may not have been so bad if you hadn't disappeared, as you'd have gotten your father's legacy. Which," he pauses to give a very European shrug, "as Aster was likewise in debt to me, is half mine."

Strider growls. I place my hand on his knee. I don't care how much or how little money is coming to me. I don't really want any part of it. With my new career and Strider, I have everything that I need. I might have been raised rich, but I'd been poorer than I'd ever believed. What's more important than money is love and family.

"Aster divided his assets between his business partner, me," he indicates himself with a grin, "and his beloved wife." He raises an eyebrow toward me.

Strider snorts. "With no will, his wife would be his only surviving beneficiary."

"And what would Bella Katrina here do with a trafficking empire? Or the whorehouses and drug dens?" He shakes his head. "Tut, tut, Strider. She couldn't have maintained control." He inclines his head toward Chaz. "You both know that and what we agreed. I'm happy to split the businesses down the middle to avoid bloodshed and ill will between us. After all, we operate in the same state."

Chaz leans forward. "Soulz get the money laundering businesses, the gun trade—"

"Yes, yes," Michael interrupts. "The more morally grey areas, as

we agreed. The ones your more sensitive souls, pun intended, can stomach." He laughs.

"And Katrina gets her father's legacy," Strider states.

"What's left after James's debts are paid, yes," Michael agrees.

"I don't want any of it."

"Then give it to charity. I don't give a fuck what you do with it."

"We'll deal with Abraham James's will first. Everything was left to you, Mrs. Aster, but as you couldn't be found, the executors sold the assets and set up a trust. That now comes to you."

I nod. Most will go to Michael in any event, but all I want to do is cast off all the shackles of my previous life and revert to being Jasmine. If I never hear the name Katrina again, I wouldn't be more happy.

"Now on to Aster's will."

Again, I tune him out as he lists all the businesses my late husband owned, slightly amused to hear them referred to by innocent-sounding names and descriptions like laundromat and bakery, and not as the fronts for *whorehouses* or *trafficking warehouses* that I now know them to be. I shudder, not wanting to think of how evil were the hands that once had touched me. If it was my decision, I'd walk away from everything my father and Barclay had left.

I know though that the Soulz are a one-percenter motorcycle club. And while the opportunity to take businesses of the type we're talking about might not appeal to me, it was a treasure trove to them. If they'd walked away from everything, they'd have appeared weak. By coming to an amicable arrangement between the Mafia and MC, they were making connections that might stand them in good future stead, allies rather than enemies.

At last, the lawyer asks, "So, any questions? In short, we're just waiting for probate, then everything will be split as I've just described."

There are no questions from me or anyone else, though Barclay might be screaming from hell that none of this was what he intended. Luckily, the lawyer has no connection with the world beyond.

We leave with polite handshakes and insincere condolences offered and accepted with the same dishonesty.

Outside, I take a lung full of blissful fresh air.

"I offer you lunch," Michael's deep, cultured voice says. "In the best Italian restaurant in town."

Strider hugs me into his side. "You'll forgive us if we have to decline."

Michael chuckles, reaches forward and takes my hand. "*Bella*, you know where to come if you ever get fed up with walking on the grey side." He chuckles at the growl that comes out of Strider's mouth.

Reclaiming my hand and placing it on the arm of my man, I tell the consigliere, "If I were ever inclined to swap grey, it wouldn't be for black."

Not suggesting he's in any way offended, Michael laughs. He raises his chin toward Strider. "You're a lucky fucking man. It's just bad luck Barclay saw her first. If I'd seen this delightful *tesoro*, I'd have claimed her for myself. And, I'd never have left her to doubt for a moment that she was the most important thing in my world."

"She is in mine," Strider pronounces. "We might have a truce, Michael, but if you step one foot over the line, I'm going to burn your fuckin' world down."

Is it wrong that my panties grow wet at his declaration? Other women might swoon at the smartly dressed, well-put-together man, but me? I prefer my rough and very tough biker.

CHAPTER TWENTY-ONE
STRIDER

I'm of two minds about our deal. I'm not sure how much Jasmine realises that if we hadn't met the Mafia halfway, she wouldn't have been mine. She'd either have been dead or promised to the devil, Michael.

Though he'd professed to despise the way Aster had treated her, I very much doubted he'd be kind. To his sort, women were objects to be played with.

I hadn't been blind to the way he'd flirted with her that day we'd listened to the wills being read. Part of me had been proud she was someone to be coveted, but the main portion of me was screaming she was mine. I might have had my head up my ass, but I'd removed it in time. I can't deny I felt relieved to see the back of Michael D'Angelo. I'd worried he wouldn't just walk away, but after three months, I've started to think he isn't just biding his time.

Part of me worries that I've played her, taken the opportunities offered because she was married into the mob. But if I, on behalf of the Soulz, hadn't played my part, neither of us might be alive.

She already knows I'm no angel, yet has agreed to stay by my side. And after what she told me last night, I know exactly where to take her.

Hopping onto the back of my bike as if she's been riding it all her life, she's happy to go wherever I do without asking for an explanation. A true biker's old lady, she looks great in her leathers and takes every opportunity to ride behind me. Maybe it's all my years in the saddle, or perhaps I've just become accustomed to the idea that fate will hit when it's your time. I've stopped worrying that I'm putting her in danger when she wraps those arms around me. Jasmine loves to ride.

Today I'm not going far, just to the mall, and to a jewellers I've often admired. She balks at the cost of the ring I know really suits her, but after a bit of persuasion, she agrees to wear the symbol that tells the citizen world she's mine.

As the proprietor goes to ring the till up, she leans into me. "I don't expect this just because I'm pregnant."

I turn to face her. "Would it help if I tell you that this is the most right thing I've ever done in my life?" I hear footsteps returning and glare at the man, who takes the hint and disappears to give us space. Placing my hands on her arms, I try to explain. "Anna and I were childhood sweethearts. Prom queen and prom king, expected to be the fairy tale story and be together all of our lives. When we got married, I said vows I thought I meant until you, Jasmine. When I admitted to myself what I felt for you, when I let my feelings override my guilt for Anna's condition, looking back, I realise I was just an actor playing a part in my first marriage. The depth of my feelings for you is so different, and part of that is how you complement me completely. Your dreams are mine, and mine yours. So I mean what I said. This feels one hundred percent right."

Tears appear in her eyes. "I was worried about getting

pregnant again so fast. Worried that that was the reason you asked me to marry you."

Placing my hand on her stomach, I reassure her, "Junior here is the icing on the cake." I pause, breathe in, then sigh out. "Fate and I haven't always been friends, you know that. But maybe there's balance, and with the downs, there are ups. This is the most amazing thing that's ever happened to me in my life. I've been given a second chance. With you. With our child."

A clearing of a throat reminds me where we are. The manager of the store is waiting, and from his hesitant expression, he's not sure if I'm going to be getting engaged or not. Putting him out of his misery, I take out my wallet and extract my card.

He can't take it and insert it into his machine fast enough, passing it over so I can put in my code before I change my mind. Jasmine vibrates at my side, and I know she's giggling, realising, like me, that he's making sure he gets his sale.

The velvet ring box goes into my pocket. I wanted her with me to choose it, but the official proposal and offering it to her will come later. Not that she knows what I've got planned.

As we go back to the bike, I warn her, "You're three months pregnant, Jas. This is the last ride on my bike."

There's a pout on her lips when she puts on her helmet, but I know she understands. I won't do anything to risk either her or the precious cargo she's carrying. In true Jasmine style though, she has the last word. "Then I hope you only want one kid, as I like riding this bike far too much."

I snort. One, ten, I'll give her however many she wants. All I need is her in my life.

Since I brought her back to the clubhouse, life's been so different, yet in many ways, just the same. Things slid back into place. The club girls stopped arguing. They and the prospects did the clean up of the clubhouse without complaining and also learned how to cook halfway decent meals. The bar always runs smoothly and is never out of stock. Brothers' differences are settled fast, with Jasmine's quick wit and interjection of comments that settle fights down. She's the perfect prez's old lady.

While I hate comparing her to Anna, my life as a brother, let alone prez, would have been so much easier if she'd played her role in the club. I'd been a fool to think I could live two separate lives. Now I have a combined one, and I couldn't be happier.

I'm going to miss her riding with me. She's a natural and somehow seems to balance the bike. As I turn into the compound, regret sweeps over me, needing me to remind myself it will only be another six months before she delivers my baby, and once she's recovered, will be able to ride once more.

In choreographed movement, she dismounts before I paddle walk the bike back into my parking space. I take her helmet, then her hand, and walk beside her into the clubhouse.

It's exactly as I'd planned. In fact, before we even enter, a child's squeals and a baby's cry betray a part of what we're going to find inside. Jasmine's startled eyes come to mine, but I don't explain anything and just push open the door.

Sheri is standing just inside with a three-year-old holding onto her hand and StoryTeller beside her with his young baby, a boy, in his arms. It's that sight that gives Jasmine a clue that I've got something planned, especially as Chaz waves his hand from over at the bar.

I drag her into the middle of the club room, and waste no time. Falling to my knees in front of her, I tell her, "Since the day you first walked into this clubhouse, you've been mine. You and everyone know that. You wear my cut, you're my ol' lady. And now I want to make you completely mine. I want to tie you to me so even the government can't take you away." I pause for the dutiful chuckles and laughs. "So, Jasmine, will you do me the honour of becoming my wife?" I pull out the ring box.

She chose the ring. She knew this was coming. Even so, it doesn't stop the tears flooding from her eyes. Pregnancy hormones? Maybe. But she sinks to the floor alongside me. "Strider, *Colt*," she adds my government name in a whisper only I can hear, "I'd be more than honoured to wear your ring and become your wife."

I slide the diamond band onto her finger, then pull her to her feet. I barely hear the cheers around us as I clasp her in my arms and lay my mouth on hers.

Once I release her, she's pulled away and hugged in turn by each of my brothers. My back is slapped so hard my skin starts to burn. Then corks pop as the champagne starts to flow.

I can't remember ever feeling any happier than this, having that sense that now everything's right in my world. It's as though I've reached the end of one journey and have embarked on another.

And this time, I won't be alone on the ride.

I'm musing on the luck that for once seems to be on my side when a throaty roar of multiple bikes sounds right outside the clubhouse. It's so close that the prospect on guard duty must have allowed them inside—or he's bleeding out at his post.

Music stops. Guns come out of holsters, and I'm pleased to see Buzz lift Jasmine into the safe area behind the bar.

The door bursts open.

Oh fuck.

Moving forward, I snarl, "I could have fuckin' killed you."

Putting away my piece, I hold out my hand. Slugger takes it, pulls me in, and slaps my back hard.

"Always good to see my boys are sharp," he tells me, which the enforcers who have accompanied him try hard to stifle their laughs.

Some things change, some things stay the same, I think to myself. Half turning, I wave my hand toward Jas, but she's already one step ahead and is emerging from behind the bar with bottles of beer on a tray.

Slugger views her up and down, his gaze landing on her long enough to earn him a growl. Ignoring me, he addresses her. "We meet at last."

Jasmine's seen him before, but as a club girl and was never introduced. Now, he's giving her the respect that is due to my old lady. I suppress a grin, easily reading that she's keeping hold of that tray like a shield, knowing Slugger's reputation with women well.

To take his focus off her, I relieve Jas of two of the beers. Handing one to him, I casually enquire, "To what do we owe this pleasure?"

Turning back to me, Slugger's mouth widens, corners turning up. "Hear you've taken on some new businesses and partnered with the Mafia, I believe?" His brow rises.

I bark a laugh. We hadn't broadcast anything, but nothing much gets past him. Shaking my head, I gesture toward my office. "Come with me. I'll fill you in."

Risking a glance back at Jasmine, I see her grinning, and gesturing with her hand as if to wave me off, totally unfazed that it's her engagement party Slugger's barged into and interrupted.

Leading the way with Slugger following, I can't keep the smile off my face. *Fucking great old lady.*

ACKNOWLEDGEMENTS AND AUTHOR'S NOTE

In early 1985, on a cold winter's morning, I broke down by the side of the road. I had no mobile phone in those days, so approached a nearby house for help. It was Limebrook Farm, a livery yard and riding stables that I didn't know at that point would, in future, become a huge part of my life.

I rang the doorbell, was hustled inside by a lovely women who had a toddler at her feet. After using the phone, I waited until help turned up. It wasn't until fifteen years later than I realised it was Sherry I'd met that day.

Fast forward to when my son was six years old and wanted to learn to ride. I took him to Limebrook as it was the nearest stables. Two years later we bought our own pony, Jazz, and kept her at livery there. By then, my husband, I, and my son would all ride.

Limebrook wasn't just business, run by the Lowes, it was a family encompassing customers and staff. We had so much fun – special ride outs, birthday and Christmas parties, summer barbeques. It became a huge part of our lives.

But Sherry became ill in 2003, and it took two years before she was diagnosed with Pick's Disease. By 2007 her illness meant the business had got too much. The riding school closed, and the farm became just a livery yard, but the sense of family and belonging survived, and became even closer. I, Steve and Michael spent the majority of our free time there until 2012, when I was made redundant and could no longer afford the livery costs. Jazz went to an amazing family on loan, but we still kept in touch and visited often.

We were, unfortunately, witness to Sherry's decline. As in Anna's story, despite all the challenges it brought, Sherry was nursed at home, included in everything even though she may not have known she was part of it.

She finally lost her battle with the disease in early 2018.

That same year that her youngest daughter—who wasn't even born that long ago day when I first met Sherry, came to my first book signing at my PA. And wow, Alex, what a great time we had there!

I've written this book with the permission of the Lowe's family, as the devastating Pick's Disease is not well known, and they thought more people should know about it.

And if you recognise the name, Alex, she's been one of my beta readers from the start, and a great supporter of my writing. I owe you even more thanks this time, Alex. I'm sorry if some of Strider's book was a painful read, and so grateful that you took the time to explain the disease to me.

Thanks also to my other amazing beta readers, Sheri, Jo and Kathy, my editor Maggie Kern, and proofreader Darlene Tallman.

Once again I've used the talent of photographer Golden Czermak for the cover photo.Victor Rahl, as model, for me brought Strider alive. The end result of the amazing cover was pulled together by CT Cover Designs.

Finally, last as always, but definitely not least, thanks to all of you, my wonderful readers who've taken a chance on this book. If it wasn't for your encouragement, I wouldn't keep writing. I have recently received messages and emails telling me how much you like my books, and I love reading everyone. A positive message inspires me to write more.

This book, like all of my works, has been to beta readers,

through editing twice, to a proofreader and then to ARC readers, but there could still be the odd typo that's crept through. Please message me if you've found anything so I have a chance to correct the book. I love to hear from readers, even if you're pointing out something I've got wrong.

If you've enjoyed this book please consider writing a review. Reviews are essential to us authors, and I appreciate and read them all.

Reader group:. https://www.facebook.com/groups/1852824718066605

Newsletter: http://eepurl.com/b1PXO5

Love and peace
Manda

Property of Saint - Kings of Anarchy MC: Arizona Book 1

My name might be Saint, but I'm more devil than angel. I don't give a damn when others live or die, unless it affects me or my club.

So what made me stop when I saw a car run off the road? And why did I lie in order to save her life?

Maybe it would have been better had I left well alone.

Rescuing her put me at odds with the rest of the Kings. To them she's the enemy. To me? She's mine.

OTHER WORKS BY MANDA MELLETT

Satan's Devils MC Boxset 2 Books 6-8

Satan's Devils MC Boxset 3 Books 9-11

Satan's Devils MC - Colorado Chapter

Paladin's Hell (#1) Paladin and Jayden

Demon's Angel (#2) Demon and Violet

Devil's Due (#3) Beef and Steph

Devil's Dilemma (#4) Pyro and Mel

Ink's Devil (#5) Ink and Beth

Devil's Spawn (#6)

Satan's Devils MC - Next Generation

Amy's Santa (#1) Wizard and Amy

Hawk's Cry (#2) Hawk and Olivia

Twisted Throttle (#3) Throttle and Gwen

Saving Marvel (#4) Marvel and Virginia

Satan's Devils MC - San Diego Chapter

Being Lost (#1)

Grumbler's Ride (#2)

Avenging Devil Part 1 (#3)

Avenging Devil Part 2 (#4)

Satan's Devils MC - Utah Chapter

Road Tripped (#1)

Stormy's Thunder (#2)

Satan's Devils MC - Las Vegas Chapter

Red's Peril - Part 1

Red's Peril - Part 2

Petty's Crimes

<u>Wicked Warriors MC - Arizona Chapter</u>

Warts an' All

Tickety Tock

<u>Wretched Soulz MC</u>

StoryTeller's Tale

Fire Meets Fire

READING ORDER

Satan's Devils MC in reading order

Turning Wheels

Drummer's Beat

Slick Running

Targeting Dart

Heart Broken

Peg's Stand

Rock Bottom

Joker's Fool

Mouse Trapped

Paladin's Hell

Blade's Edge

Demon's Angel

Devil's Due

Heart Mended (novella)

Truck Stopped

Devil's Dilemma

Ink's Devil

Devil's Spawn

Being Lost

Road Tripped

Grumbler's Ride

Stormy's Thunder

Avenging Devil Part 1

Avenging Devil Part 2

Red's Peril Part 1

Red's Peril Part 2

Petty's Crime

Second Generation

Amy's Santa

Hawk's Cry

Twisted Throtle

Saving Marvel

Wicked Warriors MC

Warts an' All

Tickety Tock

Wretched Soulz MC

StoryTeller's Tale

Fire meets Fire

Strider's Misstep

Blood Brothers (Billionaires and their bodyguards)

Stolen Lives

Close Protection

Second Chances

Identity Crisis

Dark Horses

Hard Choices

STAY IN TOUCH

Email: manda@mandamellett.com

Website: www.mandamellett.com

Sign up for my newsletter to hear about new releases in the Satan's Devils and Blood Brothers series.

Facebook reader group: https://www.facebook.com/groups/mandasbadboys/

facebook.com/mandamellett

x.com/manda_mellett

ABOUT THE AUTHOR

Manda's life's always seemed a bit weird, starting with a childhood that even today she's still trying to make sense of, then losing her parents in the late teens. Going from the tragic to the bizarre, who else could be unlucky enough to have had two car accidents, neither her fault, one involving a nun, and another involving a police woman?

There isn't enough space to list everything that's happened to Manda, or what she's learned from it. But by using the rich fabric of her personal life, psychology degree, varied work experiences, and amazing characters she's met, Manda is able to populate her books with believable in-depth characters and enjoys pitting them against situations which challenge them. Her books are full of suspense, twists and turns and the unexpected.

Manda lives in the beautiful countryside of Essex in the UK, the area's claim to fame being the Wilkin's Jam Factory at nearby Tiptree. She can usually find jars of jam which remind her of home wherever she goes. As well as writing books and reading, Manda loves walking her dogs and keeping fit. She lives with her husband of over 30 years, who, along with her son, is her greatest fan and supporter.

Manda is thankful that one of the more unusual, and at the time unpleasant, turns her life took, now enables her to spend her time writing. Confirming, in her view, every cloud has a silver lining.

Photo by Carmel Jane Photography